"Why isn't there a man in your life?"

"Maybe for the same reason there isn't a woman in yours," she replied angrily. "Farmers aren't exactly at the top of the list when it comes to romantic professions. Particularly get-dirty farmers."

"There's nothing wrong with getting dirty."

"I didn't say there was, but if the lack of a man doesn't bother me, it damn sure shouldn't bother you." She wanted to strike out, push past him, demand to know why he was leaving in June, but she was caught in his eyes, like a leaf swirling in the current of a summer river.

"Are all the men in Arkansas fools?" He touched her cheek. "Or am I so blind I can't see the flaw."

She shook her head, not trusting herself to speak.

"We're both adults, Kate. And you know I want you."

"No," she said, and heard the lack of conviction in her voice. "You're leaving—" But her words were lost in his kiss.

Dear Reader,

My husband, Glenn, and I have farmed for sixteen years now. We started with blueberries and strawberries. But it seems that the older one gets, the closer to the ground the strawberries are—or else the harder it is to bend down and weed and pick them.

So now what we have is five acres of blueberries. We talk every year about taking them out, but every year we don't, and every year come May, we go to the fields.

Farming is an insane way to make a living. It's hard physical work and you're at the mercy of the weather, bugs and the market. Harvest time is the month from hell. But it's also true that if two people can get through a harvest, they can get through anything.

Still, growing things gets in your blood, and when spring rolls around and everything turns green, your blood pumps a little faster. And when the fruit hangs so ripe and heavy that it almost hurts your eyes to look at it, when you know that all the hard work you did is right here in this cluster of blueberries or strawberries...that's when you stand out there in the field all alone with the sky and the hawks and the rabbits, and say out loud, "By God, I'm a farmer." And there's not many who can say that.

Sincerely,

Marcella Thompson

ON BLUEBERRY HILL
Marcella Thompson

Harlequin Books

TORONTO • NEW YORK • LONDON
AMSTERDAM • PARIS • SYDNEY • HAMBURG
STOCKHOLM • ATHENS • TOKYO • MILAN
MADRID • WARSAW • BUDAPEST • AUCKLAND

For all the small, independent farmers.
Guardians of the land and a way of life,
they give us a sense of who we are.

ISBN 0-373-03326-5

ON BLUEBERRY HILL

Copyright © 1994 by Marcella Thompson.

Printed in U.S.A.

PROLOGUE

Jay Thomas stood outside the hospital room for a long moment taking deep measured breaths, trying to make the smile come. Anyone passing by would think from the creases in his deeply tanned face that smiles came easily and often to this man. But not today. Groaning, he ran his fingers through a shock of windblown hair, and what finally brought the smile was the thought that the first thing his father would probably say was, "Go get a haircut."

As he reached for the door, it opened and his sister slipped out. "You look awful," she said, kissing him.

"How is he, Beth?"

"Dad's going to be fine. It's you I'm worried about." She scanned his face. "Luke's only six, Jay. He doesn't understand what's going on. Give him some time."

"Beth—"

"I know, it's none of my business, but you've *got* to find someplace to dump all that anger." She smiled and touched his cheek with a long slender hand. "Dad needs his charming, carefree 'no problem, we can handle it' son right now, not a brooding Heathcliff. And so do I."

He watched her walk down the hall, then forced the smile again and opened the door. The shades were drawn against the bright California sun and he blinked at the darkness. "You're going to turn into a mole, Dad."

"A mole would be a hell of a lot prettier sight than me," Luther Thomas said in a halting voice.

Jay swallowed hard. His father's face was in shadow, but it was clear in Jay's mind. The slight drooping of the left side of the face, the crooked smile on the rare occasions Jay or Beth could coax a smile. "A few months of rehab and the doctor says you'll be as good as new." *If we can make him want it bad enough to go through the pain,* the doctor had added.

"Rehab designed by Edgar Allen Poe." Luther turned his face toward the wall. "You need a haircut."

Jay's smile was fleeting, for he was concerned by the change in his father's personality. Luther Thomas had always been a man who'd liked the long odds. He'd expanded their winery when other wineries were folding, planted more vineyards when other owners were plowing theirs up for condos. "You're as tough as nails, you can take it," Jay said, trying to will Luther's zest for life back into him, trying to make the old frail look go away. Luther told him he should be at the farm pruning, not hanging around the hospital ward.

Jay tensed, then forced himself to relax. "The new owner took possession this morning. It's his problem now." The sale of the vineyard had finalized the property settlement, finalized Jay's divorce.

He and Beth and Luther had sold the family winery to a conglomerate back in May. They hadn't been looking to sell, but the offer was too good to refuse, and Luther, still reeling from his wife's death the year before, said it was a good time to move on. Two weeks later, Jay was served with divorce papers. Jennifer couldn't touch the proceeds from the family corporation, so she went after the vineyard she and Jay owned jointly. Now *it* was gone, along with his son.

"You get things worked out about little Lukie?"

"No." The last thing Jay wanted to talk about was the divorce or Jennifer—or how little he would see of Luke. He rubbed the back of his neck till it hurt.

"We could both go out to Arkansas, son. Get that farm ready for the harvest." Luther coughed. "There's a woman for you. *She's* not afraid of a little dirt and sweat."

"Dad, I'm not in the market. Not now, not ever, okay? And we'll see about the harvest in Arkansas."

After the winery sale, Luther had taken a vacation and come back to California in September with the news that he had bought a blueberry farm in Arkansas. The logic of which no one, least of all Jay, could begin to understand. "Arkansas?" Jay had asked. "It's beautiful out there," Luther had said. "A man's got room to breathe."

Luther hitched himself up in the hospital bed. "I bought that place on a lease-purchase. If I don't take care of it, it'll go back to the Harmons."

A bad move as far as Jay was concerned. He read it as a way for the Harmons to take Luther's hefty down payment and cancel the option because of a few weeds. Luther said it was common practice back there, to protect the mortgage holder. That it made Leonard Harmon feel better because it didn't sound so final. "You're too young to understand that, son," Luther had said.

But Jay understood loss all too well.

Luther took a deep breath. "They love that place."
The raspy hollow sound of his voice tore at Jay's
heart. "Send Kate Harmon twenty thousand dollars,
tell her I've been delayed, tell her to hire a good farm
manager until I get there." He put an arm over his
eyes. "Don't tell her about the stroke. She'd worry."

"I'll take care of it, Dad. Quit worrying and get
well. Then you can go and oversee the harvest yourself." The farm in Arkansas was the only thing that
sparked any interest in Luther since the stroke, but Jay
doubted his father would be able to manage any kind
of business again, let alone a farm. He started to say
something else, but Luther had dozed off. Stepping to
the bed, he brushed a strand of hair from his father's
brow. "I love you," he whispered.

CHAPTER ONE

SOME YEARS, late February turned gentle in north-west Arkansas, coaxing the daffodils and grape hyacinths from their long winter sleep too early, causing the peach trees to stir and think about blooming long before it was prudent. As Kate Harmon bent to prune a particularly tough blueberry cane, she knew they would pay for the seemingly endless days of sunshine and the hard bright sky so blue it made you squint to look at it. It was the kind of day to put on some shorts and run through the fields until you weren't cold anymore. Which she might have done if George Hartley, her hired man, hadn't been working two rows over. George was in his late sixties and of the opinion that farming was serious work and a field no place for frivolity. George was the only man in the world who could still make Kate feel like a five-year-old.

As she wrestled the cane out, Chester and Molly, her two black Labs, stood quivering with anticipation. "How do you expect us to ever get the pruning done when I have to play fetch with you guys?" she asked and threw the cane. The Labs were on it in a flash, each tugging for possession. Kate's two kittens deserted a beetle they had unearthed and attacked Chester's tail with enthusiasm.

"One of these days he's going to turn around and eat you two," she said to the kittens, not believing it any more than they did. Chester had found the kittens on New Year's Day, huddled together in a patch of tall weeds out by the county road that ran past the farm. Kate had taken them home.

Two rows over, George grumbled that the work might be easier if the dogs would learn to haul the canes to the brush pile instead of shredding them. George had lived on a farm down the road all his life and worked for the Berry Patch since the first blueberry plant was put in the ground fourteen years before.

"Good luck," Kate said, and stretched. She was tall and had the lean healthy body of a woman who gets her exercise out in the sun, instead of in a gym. Despite, or perhaps because of, her relationship with the earth and growing things, she seemed to have a perpetual look of wonder etched in her face—guileless, calm, serene, quick to smile. Her honey-blond hair had darkened a shade over the winter, but would turn the color of sunshine again by July. Her winter-pale skin would become a rich bronze, giving her deep blue eyes a touch of violet.

"Don't seem the same without Leonard, does it?" George asked this question every day. "Reckon him and Sarah are playin' on some beach in Florida while we're up here doin' the work." George always tried to sound disapproving, but it invariably came out sounding more like a mixture of curiosity and disbelief that anyone could possibly prefer a place like Florida over Arkansas.

Kate smiled. She suspected her father was pacing rather than playing, driving her mother crazy worrying about whether they'd been right to sell the farm—the big blueberry farm that adjoined hers. The decision to sell had been a hard one for her parents, harder yet to sign the papers, get in the motor home and drive south. But after her father's heart attack the doctor had been adamant about the amount of work Leonard should do—and not do. Still, there were times when Kate wondered if her father would ever adjust to a life without blueberries. She had dreamed of one day buying her parents' place and combining it with hers but, well, it was better this way. For everyone.

George examined the bush she had just pruned. "Gonna be a right good crop this year," he said, counting the tiny fruit buds the plant had set back in late fall.

Kate knew they were going to have one of those incredible harvests that only happened once every five or ten years. George knew that, too, but he was not one to get excited until the crop was hanging blue and ready to pick.

"Get past the bud worms and late freezes and spring storms and it's easy pickin's," he mused. "Seems a shame for Leonard to miss a crop like this." George was having as much trouble dealing with her father's absence as she was, although he'd never admit it.

"They'll be back for the harvest." Her father would help with her two acres of strawberries and five acres of blueberries, which was a far cry from the responsibility of harvesting thirty-five acres of blueberries on the big farm. No heavy lifting, no all-night driving to market. Just a little supervising and mowing and puttering around with his beloved machinery—all under the watchful eye of her mother.

The burning question that kept Kate awake at night was where to find a competent manager to handle the big farm. Luther Thomas had sent her a huge check in

January and a brief—very brief—note saying that he'd been delayed, that the money was to hire a good farm manager. She had advertised, put out the word to other blueberry growers, interviewed a long string of ex-hippies, would-be back-to-the-landers and really nice young men who had never even raised a garden but thought they would like to try, and she had come up empty. If her father returned and found nobody minding the store, he might—no, he *would*—have apoplexy.

She sent Luther a letter in early February, telling him she was looking for "just the right man," but not to worry, they would work out something about the harvest. It sounded easy if she said it fast enough. She wiggled a slender cutting at the kittens. "I just hope Mr. Thomas is here in time for the pruning."

George flexed his shoulders. "He does need to get a move on. I hope he's not plannin' on us doin' it for him."

She hadn't told George about Luther's letter, knowing it would worry him to death. It was bad enough she was worrying herself to death about it. She wished Luther had been a bit more specific about when he planned to arrive—before she had to admit she couldn't find him a manager would be nice. He'd certainly been adamant in September that he would be here to learn the pruning, the spraying, every aspect of the business. "I'm sure he'd be more than happy to hire you to help."

"I'm gettin' too old for this kind of work, Katie."

"You've been saying that for as long as I can remember."

"Gettin' truer ever' year. Why don't you just hitch up with that Wade boy and quit all this hard work?"

"Barry Wade is a good friend, George. That's all."
George pointed out that was *her* side of the story.
"Well, that's the only side that counts as far as I'm
concerned."

She wasn't about to let him go into why she should
have married Barry Wade years ago. Or for that matter why she should marry him now. Barry had grown
up down the road. At age seven, he had announced to
both families that he was going to marry Kate. He was
a wildly successful lawyer these days and still announced at family gatherings that he intended to
marry her, convinced that if he waited long enough she
would weaken. She was tempted at times, although she
had a feeling it would scare the living daylights out of
Barry if she ever said yes. She suspected that it was a
fantasy he kept alive because he'd lived with it for so
long, but that deep down, that was all it was. As for
herself, she loved Barry dearly, but she didn't love him
the way she wanted to love the man she'd marry. "I'm
good for a few more years of work, George."

"A few more years and you'll be broke down."
George was of the opinion that hard work was good
for a man but made a woman old before her time. And
at twenty-six, Kate, he judged, was almost over the
hill—if she was to find a husband, she'd have to find
him soon. "Speakin' of which, I'm goin' home for
dinner and a nap," he said, ambling off toward his old
truck.

Kate could tell his arthritis was bothering him.
"Stay home. We'll start again tomorrow," she called.

The sun was warm and the house seemed too far
away as she unzipped her coverall and stripped off her
stocking cap. Her hair fell loose, and the gentle breeze
that brushed her cheeks told her the temperature might

hit the high fifties before the day was out. The geese
would come soon. She would hear them first, then
watch as a V of whirring wings swept over the farm.
If she was lucky, they would bank and come back and
settle noisily on the lake to rest for the night before
starting the next leg of their flight to Canada, their
bellies full of grain she kept just on the off chance they
might stop.

She flopped down. The ground was dry and rea-
sonably warm for this time of the year, the grass thick
and soft between the rows, just beginning to show
signs of greening. She stretched out on her back and
watched a red-tailed hawk ride a thermal high above.
George would have a fit if he ever caught her napping
in the field, but to Kate, it was the most glorious napping spot in the world—at least until the bugs came
out. Chester went off to look for rabbits, but Molly
sighed and settled down with her head on Kate's legs.

"Nap time, Molly," she said and slipped the head-
phones of her cassette player into place. Willie Nelson filled her ears as she wondered what her parents
were doing at that moment. As Molly groaned and
squirmed to settle herself, the kittens appeared from
nowhere and curled up on Kate's stomach. She stroked
their soft fuzzy coats and felt their rapid purrs vibrate
through her body as she tightened and relaxed her sore
muscles. About the time her body got used to pruning, the season was over.

It was the first year she had ever pruned without her
father on the other side of the row, and she missed him
more than she cared to think about. She was glad her
parents were out from under the work of the farm, and
she wanted them to have this time in their life to do the
things they'd dreamed of. She'd never even hinted that

she wanted to buy the big farm herself. Her father would have worried himself silly, then given it to her, then stayed to help—and probably killed himself in the process.

A line of orange-flagged stakes now separated the two properties, the old fence having come down when she'd bought her farm. She'd talked to Luther Thomas about putting up another fence, thinking it the proper thing to do, but he had been insulted. "Good neighbors don't need fences," he'd said.

Kate closed her eyes and watched the patterns of light swirl like a kaleidoscope on the backs of her eyelids, listened to Willie's tale of the redheaded stranger and fell asleep.

At some point she felt Molly stir and thought she heard Chester bark, but paid them little mind. They were much more interested in barking at birds and rabbits and frogs than at humans. When she felt a gentle pressure on her shoulder, she swatted at it. "Go chase a rabbit, Chester," she muttered.

The kittens stirred, then were quiet. Something touched her shoulder again, more insistently this time, and she put an arm over her face to avoid the wet tongue she knew would come next. "Go away, Chester!"

"I'm not Chester," a voice said. "I'm looking for Kate Harmon."

The voice gave a hard edge to her name, and Kate's eyes flew open. She was looking—upside down—at a pair of mirrored aviator glasses.

"I thought maybe you were dead," the man said in a mocking voice. "You look rather ceremonial, all laid out with your faithful companions."

She pulled off the earphones, dumped the kittens and stood up in an easy fluid motion. "I... I'm Kate Harmon, and I was..." She smiled and waved at the ground, trying to shake the sleep away. The man didn't smile back, didn't say anything. "You here about the job?"

He looked beyond her, taking in the blueberry fields. "I guess you could say that. Do you spend your nights out here, too? Or just naps?"

He made it sound like an indiscretion. "I don't... no. I mean, it's such a gorgeous day and the kittens were tired and..." Her eyes narrowed as she studied the man. He stood with his hands in the back pockets of faded jeans. A gray hooded sweatshirt hung open, revealing a maroon T-shirt covering a broad chest. He was tall and wide-shouldered, his black hair long and ruffled, his face all angles beneath several days' growth of dark stubble. His work boots were old and worn. *He's been on the road,* she thought, pushing away the fantasy that came full-blown and unbidden into her mind—an ancient warrior tossed down from a storm cloud.

She smiled, realizing here was a man who looked as if he knew how to work. "What kind of farm experience do you have?" Molly ambled over to the man and began nuzzling his legs and boots. Kate pushed her fingers through her hair and leaves cascaded out.

"I'm..." He frowned and glanced away from her. "What kind of experience are you looking for?"

Kate felt more comfortable now that they were talking about business, instead of naps. "Commercial ag, preferably orchards or landscape crops, since blueberry culture is kind of in-between. In my wildest dreams, somebody from Michigan who actually knows what a blueberry plant is.''

''Grapes?''

''Blueberries are more like orchards.'' Grapes would be fine if in fact he knew anything about them.

He took off the sunglasses and gazed out over the fields. ''They're permanent plantings,'' he said with an arrogant shrug. ''They need fertilizer, water and sunshine.''

She ignored the shrug and the even more arrogant answer. She'd learned early on to cull the want-to-be's from the actually-done-its. ''Irrigation systems?''

''I would assume shallow roots, so low-pressure in-line. Emitter every two feet, half-gallon per hour,'' he said, turning back to face her.

Kate found herself looking into eyes the color of oak leaves in the spring, eyes so intense her list of questions flew off on the gentle breeze. ''References?'' she asked quickly.

''I…'' He turned away to examine the swollen fruit buds on a blueberry plant. ''No.''

She wasn't sure if it was her imagination or what, but he seemed suddenly reluctant, as if trying to make up his mind about something. *Probably can't stand the thought of working for a woman,* she thought. ''Well, I'd prefer to check a couple of references. And I'm sure you'd like to check me out,'' she said with a note of sarcasm.

The eyes that inspected her from head to foot flickered with anger—and something else. ''I might just do that,'' he said in a low voice.

Kate's own anger swelled. ''While you're at it, you might read up on the finer points of applying for a job.''

"Forget it," he snapped, and walked away, his hands jammed in his back pockets.

As she watched him stalk off, turning every few steps to take in the farm, she could almost feel the tension and anger radiating from him. By the time she gathered her cap, her loppers and the kittens and started for the house, he was coming back, his long strides eating up the distance. "If he punches me out," she said to Chester, "bite him." But the man stopped some distance away. The sunglasses covered his eyes again, but he gave her a ghost of a smile.

"Work me for a week," he said softly, stripping off the glasses. "See what you think."

Kate swallowed hard. "It pays a thousand a month and a place to live," she said softly, wondering what had happened to "Fat chance, buster," aghast that she was hiring a stranger—an arrogant angry stranger at that. But she *was* desperate and she could always fire him. Besides, she was a great believer in eyes and, my, did he have good eyes. She forced herself to look away from them. "If the harvest is good, you get a bonus."

"Fair enough," he said, coming closer. "First week's on me. I'm Jay."

His handshake was firm, which came second to eyes on Kate's judge-of-character scale. It was also very warm and sure and...nice. "I'm Kate. I'll show you where to put your things."

Thirty minutes later, Kate was on her way back to her own place, having left Jay whatever-his-name-was at one of the trailers that housed the big farm's summer workers. She couldn't believe she didn't even know his last name. More to the point, she couldn't believe she had hired a total stranger with no references. He could be a bank robber for all she knew. Or a homicidal maniac. He'd said absolutely nothing, except to ask where to find a grocery store and tell her he'd pay to have a phone put in. But he'd taken in every detail of the farm, and of *her*. At least, she supposed he was looking at her behind those stupid sunglasses.

Lord, what have I done? she wondered. The dogs trotted happily beside her, and the kittens bounded ahead, stopping now and then to pounce on bugs. "What are you guys so happy about?" she complained. "We'll probably be murdered in our beds." It was hard to believe a murderer could have such beautiful eyes, but one could never tell. By the time she opened her front door, she was thinking of ways to get rid of him—tactfully.

She gave the dogs their after-work dog bones, fed the kittens and reheated the breakfast coffee. "It's a beautiful day out there, Snit," she said to the calico cat lounging on the kitchen table. "You ought to try it sometime." The cat yawned and reached out to snag her as she walked by. Kate sidestepped. "You don't need to eat. You haven't done anything to burn off breakfast yet."

Snit was an enormous cat, old, elegant and crotchety, who ruled the house with terrorist tactics. She never hurt the other animals, but they treated her as if she might start at any minute. She reminded Kate of some aging queen who governs her subjects with an iron hand, and while visitors gave the cat a wide berth, Kate rather respected the calico for being such a curmudgeon.

She turned on the answering machine. "Kate, honey, can you bring something with blueberries to the meeting tomorrow night?'' Gladys, her neighbor across the road, was hosting the Extension Homemakers' meeting this month. Kate always went, not because of the programs, but because she loved the neighborhood ladies who made up the club. ''And Clara's sick,'' the message went on. ''Could you do a program on healthy after-school snacks?'' Kate laughed. The average age of the club was at least seventy.

The tone sounded. ''Kate, how come you haven't called? We're supposed to have pizza this week.''

Barry had moved back to the Wade farm after his parents died, built a new house and begun raising registered Angus cattle. They had remained best friends through the years. Pizza meant he had a new girlfriend, and Kate would have to suffer through not only all the lurid details of the romance, but a lecture on how it was all her fault for not marrying him.

Kate turned on the news and cooked a hamburger, but as she sat in front of the television, she was thinking not about world events, but of the strange man she had hired—a man with eyes the color of oak leaves in the spring.

CHAPTER TWO

THE FIRST THING Kate did every morning was throw on a robe and take her first cup of coffee out to the front porch. As a farmer, she was an avid weather watcher and always knew what was predicted, but liked to see it for herself each morning. She would then retire to the kitchen for cereal, lots of strong coffee and yesterday's crossword puzzle. After that, she was ready for her day's work.

This morning, however, she had company. Jay was sitting on the steps watching the eastern sky turn pink as if this was something he did every morning—on her porch. "What are you doing here?" she squeaked.

He looked up at her. He was clean shaven, his hair still damp from the shower. "You hired me, remember?"

"Oh. Right. Well…" Kate was barely coherent until she had coffee. "It's not light enough to work yet."

His eyes wandered up her robe to her tousled hair. "It probably will be by the time you get ready."

She pulled her robe tighter, supposing she should offer him some coffee. But dammit, she didn't want her morning routine ruined. And she had no intention of traipsing out to the field in the dark. "I haven't had my coffee yet, so… You'll find loppers in that big shed over there. Grab some you like and I'll be along."

He gave her a look that clearly indicated what he thought of farmers who weren't in the fields by the crack of dawn.

She retreated into the house, feeling guilty that she hadn't been up for hours. Which was annoying, not to mention stupid, since it wasn't light enough to see the bushes. The dogs, still piled on the couch, thumped their tails but didn't stir. "Great watchdogs," she scolded. "I could be carried off in my sleep and you wouldn't even notice."

Twenty minutes later, after two quick cups of coffee and no cereal or crossword, she grabbed her loppers, marshaled the dogs and kittens and set out for the shed on the big farm, her mood far from cheerful.

The morning was frosty and still. Wisps of mist rose off the lake, hanging for long moments before the morning swallowed them. Beyond the lake, a heavy trail of fog marked the winding river. Kate loved this time before the sun popped over the treeline. The world was clean and new and the birds seemed to fall quiet in anticipation of a new day—but she hardly noticed it this morning. She stopped at the strawberry field and dug gently into the crown of a plant to see if the warm days had persuaded the plants to break dormancy. She found no signs of life yet, but the buds would come soon if the unseasonable weather continued.

She walked into the long metal building that served as both farms' packing shed during harvest and equipment storage during the winter. It was dim in the early-morning light and cold enough to turn her breath to vapor. Her new worker was nowhere to be seen. The dogs sniffed the air a few times and tore off into the fields to terrorize the rodent population. Kate was about to leave when she heard creakings from the mechanical harvester. Either rats or Jay, she concluded. As she started in that direction, Jay emerged from the bowels of the machine.

"A lot like a grape harvester except for the insides. You harvest everything with this?" he asked, walking around the machine.

"No. We hand-harvest until the fresh-market price drops, then we go in with the harvester for freezer pack." She watched him climb the ladder on the side of the machine with the easy grace of a cat going up a tree. As he examined the hydraulics and driver controls, she got the distinct impression he knew exactly what he was doing.

"Has it been modified?"

"Yeah. It's an old one. Dad fixed it up and put the new kind of slappers in it." The harvester was an enormous machine that looked more like something out of a science-fiction movie than a piece of farm equipment. It waddled through the fields, straddling a row of blueberries, shaking the bushes gently with plastic slappers. The ripe berries fell onto conveyer belts that carried them back to a platform and dumped them into bright yellow field lugs.

Jay glanced at her from the driver's seat ten feet above. "What happens to the leaves and debris?"

His face was in shadow, his expression unreadable. For some reason, seeing him sitting up there made her feel...funny. Caffeine withdrawal, she thought. "The berries go through a blower, wet line, get sized, dried and packed in thirty-pound boxes." She kicked the harvester's nearest tire. Had she been lucky enough to hire someone who could actually run this monster? It was the one piece of equipment she'd never operated. Although she'd ridden on it with her father, she never felt comfortable with it. "You ever operate a grape harvester?"

"Grew up on one." He came down the ladder. "You use it for *your* berries? This is two separate farms. Right?"

"Right." Somehow she had ended up flattened against the cold metal side of the harvester, trapped unless she wanted to climb over the tractor—or Jay. "The tail end of the crop," she said, trying to ignore his closeness, the clean sharp smell of his soap and his after-shave. "Dad and I shared the equipment. The new owner liked that." The lake, which provided irrigation water for both farms, was on her land. It would cost Luther a fortune to drill an irrigation well; it would cost her a fortune to buy all new equipment. They had decided equipment and water was a good trade.

"Sounds like a good deal for you."

The obvious sarcasm in his voice made her bristle. The business of the farm was none of his business. "It's a good deal for *both* of us," she snapped and pushed past him out into the bright cold morning. "I have the water," she added. "Did you find some loppers?"

He followed, loppers in hand. "The water?"

"The water." She felt better out of the confines of the shed and supposed she'd imagined all those strange feelings. "We'll start on the Collins," she said. "They're an early variety, easy to learn on." She scooped up the kittens and tucked them inside her coverall. When she straightened, Jay was staring at her front, which now bulged and squirmed as the kittens tried to escape. For a moment she thought she detected the shadow of a smile, but he squashed it in favor of his usual expression—grim.

She found herself thinking that his smile would probably be as nice as his eyes. Then her bosom gave a final lurch and two kitten heads popped out of her coverall. "Well it's a long way to the fields when you have short legs," she muttered. She marched off, lecturing Jay on the whys and wherefores of pruning blueberries as they walked.

"I'll work with you awhile, and when you get through the Collins, I'll tell you about the other four varieties," she said.

Stopping at the first row, Kate unloaded the kittens, then showed Jay the fruit buds and quickly cut out three old canes. "See the difference?"

"Uh-huh." He moved to the next bush and tapped two canes with the tip of the loppers. "These?"

"Right." He cut them and tossed the canes aside. "Then you look at it. See this one?" She pointed to a brushy cane in the center of the plant. "You could take it out or leave it till next year. Until you get the hang of it, conservative is good." She cut the cane and stepped back. "That's nice."

He circled a bush. "So how long does it take to prune all of this?" he asked.

"We did some summer pruning last year, so we won't take a lot out this time. Maybe two months if you get good."

Chester and Molly came flying down the row and stood quivering in front of Jay. "Go chase a rabbit, guys," she scolded. They flicked an ear in her direction but stared intently as Jay reached to cut a large cane.

"Are they getting ready to attack or something?"

"Ignore them."

He cut the cane and Chester whimpered. "You want to tell me what they want?" he asked with obvious amusement. "It's hard to concentrate with all this heavy breathing."

Kate sighed. "They want you to throw it."

He flung the cane down the row and the dogs sailed after it. "How long does pruning take when the dogs help?"

Kate felt her neck flush beneath her coverall. "Sometimes forever."

She settled into the rhythm of the job—bend, cut, pull, toss. Jay took on a slower rhythm, but she could tell he would get faster. She could also tell he understood plants and fruit-set and all the other things that made for a good pruner. As they worked down the row, he seemed to draw into himself, into the kind of silence she recognized as best left undisturbed. She sneaked a look at him from time to time, but he gave his full attention to the bushes, as if he was in the field alone.

"What in the world you doin' out here? I nearly knocked the house down poundin' on the door."

Kate's head snapped up at the sound of George's voice. She should have called and told him to stay home. That would have given her time to think up some explanation of why she'd hired a man she knew absolutely nothing about. "Hi, George. This is Jay, uh..."

"Thomas." Jay stuck out his hand.

"George Hartley. You any kin to Clarence Thomas?"

"No, I—"

"Name sure rings a bell," George mused, scratching his head. "Well, shoot, that's the name of the guy who bought this place. You any kin to him?"

Jay turned to throw another cane for the dogs. "Phone book's full of us."

"Kind of a funny coincidence, isn't it?" Kate said, anxious to latch onto any distraction. Jay just shrugged and bent to his work. "Right," she said. "Jay's going to be working here, George. Get the place in shape for the other Mr. Thomas."

George examined the pruned bushes. "Where you from? You look like you're from California." George was convinced he could always spot a Californian, being a great believer that they were all Okies and Arkies who had gone West during the drought and come back rich and uppity.

Jay muttered something that sounded like a yes.

"Hmm. Don't grow these things in California."

Kate sighed. If she didn't intervene, George would launch an all-day interrogation. He was as protective of the two farms as a mother hen. "He's doing fine, George," she said. "Let's get back to where we stopped yesterday."

George frowned. "You go on over, missy. I think I'd best stay here and make sure the boy's doin' it right. Leonard wouldn't want these plants messed up." He made a pruning error sound like child abuse.

Jay frowned and the muscles in his jaw tightened. Kate doubted he was accustomed to being called boy. And it was no use trying to explain that George referred to everyone under fifty as boy or missy. She took George's arm. "I'll check on him later. Jay, come get me if you have any questions," she said over her shoulder as she herded George back to her farm. The dogs raced ahead and she knew she should carry the kittens, but she wasn't about to go through *that* scene again. They could find their own way.

"Where'd he come from?" George asked.

"He applied for the job. Lots of grape experience."

"What good'll that do us? You know anything about him?"

"Mr. Thomas wanted me to hire someone till he gets here, and at least this man knows what a farm is."

"That remains to be seen, missy." After a moment, the import of what she had said hit George. "You never told me he wanted somebody hired."

"I didn't want to worry you. It's either Jay or us, and I'm not going to prune that farm." But her curiosity was piqued. Jay knew about farm equipment, about plants. He was quick, obviously well educated and well spoken—when he said anything. So who was he? And what was he doing here, instead of in California pruning grapes? They were questions to which she intended to get some answers.

As soon as George went to lunch, she walked back to the big farm. She examined Jay's work with a critical eye, but found little to criticize. She might take out this cane or that one, but for the most part he was doing as good a job as she would have. In fact, he was doing a super job, considering it was his first day. He walked up the row to meet her.

"Do I pass?"

She imagined he was mocking her, but his face showed about as much expression as a stone. "You're doing fine. It's hard to believe you've never pruned blueberries before."

"They're nice plants to work with."

"I could fix you a sandwich." Lunch seemed like a good opportunity to get some answers.

"I picked up some things last night."

"Oh. Uh, you need to stop by the house sometime and fill out some forms—I-9, W-4, that stuff." He nodded as if he knew all about that sort of paperwork.

So much for answers and small talk. "Fine. Well, I'll see you later." As she cut back across the field she knew, although she wasn't about to turn around and check it out, that Jay was standing where she'd left him, watching her. She could almost feel his eyes burning into the back of her coverall. Why was she so damned uncomfortable around him? He hadn't said or done one thing to make her feel that way, but there was something about him—his eyes, his scent, his soft easy voice... She shook herself and hurried to the house to fix a blueberry cream-cheese pie for the meeting that night and to worry about Jay Thomas.

WHEN KATE WALKED into Gladys Stanberry's house that evening, she hugged her neighbors and surrendered the pie to Mary Beth Pond. The ladies inquired about the berries and her parents, but she knew they were all dying to ask about the young man they'd seen wandering around. Not that she'd been spying on him. She had just happened to look out her kitchen window after lunch and seen him walking down the road. But if *she'd* seen him, *everyone* had seen him. Kate had lived in this area all her life, but it still amazed her how the neighborhood women knew what was happening almost before it happened.

"Kate, honey, this pie looks scrumptious," Gladys said.

Kate smiled, not daring to reveal the fact that she'd used a store-bought crust. "I'm desperate to get rid of the blueberries in my freezer. Anybody need some?" Several of the women were widows on fixed incomes and the expensive fruit strained their budgets, though they'd never admit it, just as they'd never accept fresh berries during the picking season. "Heavens no," they'd say, "you sell those berries." So each year before harvest, she gave away—or sold at bargain-basement prices—what she had in the freezer.

"I could use a few," one of her neighbors said.

"Done." And Kate took orders until Gladys herded everyone into the living room for the program. Kate knew no one was interested in her five minutes on healthy after-school snacks, but they were all great believers in going through the prescribed ritual of the meeting. Most of the Cooperative Extension Service's material was aimed at young homemakers. This group was well past that stage, and the club was more of an excuse to eat and visit than anything else. But the ladies were of a generation that needed an excuse to do that. The club served the purpose, so they dutifully presented the programs sent to them each month.

"There's a quilting workshop next week at the electric co-op. Anyone interested?" Gladys asked. No one was, so they moved on to the food. The kitchen table sagged with pies, hot rolls, fried chicken, vegetables and casseroles. Enough, Kate calculated, to feed a large family for a month. She loaded up a plate and retired to a card table in the den. Mary Beth and Gladys followed shortly.

"Whoever is that nice young man who's been wandering around your blueberries?" Mary Beth asked immediately.

"I was in my iris bed this very noon," Gladys said, "and he came right in the gate and spoke just as nice as could be. I thought you said the new owner was old, Kate."

"He is. This is just a guy I hired to help out till the owner gets here," Kate said nonchalantly, not really wanting to delve into the subject of Jay with the ladies.

Mary Beth winked at Kate. "If I were you, I'd snatch him up before he knew what hit him. Not many like that running around loose." Mary Beth and Gladys had been trying to get Kate married off for years.

"Good grief, you two. I just hired him yesterday. Besides, I'm not interested. In him or anyone else."

"Oh, pooh," Gladys said. "The right one hasn't come along. Though Lord knows it's not from lack of trying on my part. *This* one is lovely. Nice eyes and very knowledgeable about irises."

Kate had at one time resented the ladies' efforts to find her a husband, but took it in stride now, knowing it was well meant. "He'll only be here a few months."

Gladys sighed. "There I was on my knees in the Titan's Glory—those big blue-purple ones—and this voice speaks up behind me, just as soft and nice as a kitten's belly. I looked up and I swear, I thought I must be at the pearly gates. Why, I haven't seen a man like that since my Frank came courting." Gladys's husband Frank had died some ten years ago. "We had the nicest visit. He's from California and his name's Jay." Gladys rolled the name out as long as she could, obviously knowing it was a tidbit no one else had until this minute. "Jay is *so* California sounding."

Kate smiled tensely and picked up a chicken leg.

"He asked all sorts of questions," Gladys continued as conversation stopped at the other card tables.

Kate's smile stiffened in place. "What sort of questions?"

"Oh, how long everybody's lived here, and all about your folks." Gladys paused. "And which way the prevailing winds blow."

"Prevailing winds?" Kate asked.

"Yes, dear, winds." She winked at Kate. "And naturally the conversation turned to you. I told him everything he needed to know."

Kate felt her meal rumble uneasily in her stomach. "Great." She figured by now her farm manager would be long gone, afraid of being roped, tied and dragged to the altar by Gladys and crew. If he stayed, obviously Jay would have no trouble charming the ladies of the neighborhood—but why all the questions? She deftly changed the conversation, and half an hour later pleaded an early morning and went home.

Her last thought before sleep took her was, *Prevailing winds?*

CHAPTER THREE

KATE SAT at the kitchen table working on a list of packing supplies for the coming season. A cold front had swept through that morning, dragging lower temperatures and a cold drizzle behind it. The weatherman promised sunshine in a day or two, so she called George and told him it was too nasty to work. He grumbled that they would still be pruning when the berries were ripe, but Kate was determined to look after his arthritis even if he wasn't. The worst part of a day off was that tomorrow George would relate—in lurid detail—the scandalous goings-on in the afternoon talk shows.

She hadn't gone over to check on Jay. Surely he had enough sense to stay inside on a day like this.

The kitchen was a mess, crowded with books, favorite pieces of pottery, pots of parsley and basil, old iron skillets—all things she meant to straighten up and organize one day. The dogs were sprawled by the wood stove that separated the kitchen from the living room. The kittens were, as best she could tell from the noises, destroying the upstairs. Snit lay stretched out on the kitchen counter looking for all the world as if she was dead. A very elegant dead.

Kate yawned and gave serious thought to abandoning her least favorite part of farming in favor of bed and a good book. Instead, she made more coffee, hoping caffeine would keep her at the tedious details of trying to figure out the number of pints and quarts and shipping flats she should order. And there were all the supplies for the big farm. She'd promised Luther she'd do the calculations, but should she do the ordering? The money he'd sent would pay for part of his supplies, but not all. Maybe she should drop him a note.

She was strangely restless and knew it had to do with Jay Thomas. She'd hardly seen him for three days. He was in the field when she went out, still there when she left. She inspected his progress each day, tried to talk to him, but he only asked her if he was doing everything right and went on working, as if she was intruding into some secret and private world. So she checked on him and felt funny a lot and that was that.

It was great that she didn't have to supervise him, but annoying that he was so... uncommunicative. What good was another hand if you couldn't talk to him? Jay pruned as if it was some sort of sacred mission, instead of a tedious job. Once, when he was unaware of her approach, she'd watched him for a long moment and sensed in his quick efficient movements an anger so raw she couldn't begin to comprehend it. Which increased her curiosity a hundredfold. Who was he and what was he doing in Arkansas? In the night before sleep came, she conjured up all sorts of possibilities. His family wiped out in a plane crash. He was running from the law. His gorgeous wife and children kidnapped by terrorists and brutally slain. He was the ne'er-do-well son of a wealthy family. Or last but not least, he was just plain old garden-variety weird and antisocial.

Mary Beth, who worked in the county assessor's office, had called last night, all a-twitter, to tell her he'd been at the courthouse looking at aerial maps. Mary Beth had further speculated—after leaving her desk to see where he'd gone, which turned out to be the county judge's office, for what reason Mary Beth couldn't imagine—that Jay was probably a wealthy investor planning to buy all their properties for outrageous prices and that he was working undercover to get the lay of the land, so to speak. Kate didn't believe a word of it. On the other hand, she didn't particularly like the sound of it, either, although she couldn't say why. For all she knew he might be thinking about buying a place and settling in the area. Which made her feel even funnier.

The phone rang and it was Barry. "Katie, my sweet, where have you been keeping yourself? I've worn out my 'auto redial' calling you."

"Sorry, I've been busy. Slaving away in the fields."

"You should have gone to law school. Crime is much more reliable and profitable. Listen, I was taking a deposition at the hospital and there's this nurse in orthopedics. I think it's love. You want pizza tonight?"

"You're not in love again?" Barry fell in love at least twelve times a year. Kate thought it had to do with the phases of the moon. "Okay, pizza, and you can tell me all about her."

"Well, don't sigh so much. One word from you and I would sweep you out of your drudgery and turn your place into a brood farm for Herefords. Did I tell you I'm thinking about crossbreeding my Angus with Hereford?"

"No, you didn't, and not on my farm, fellow."

They set the time and Kate went back to her supply order. She was deep into figuring out quart baskets for the strawberries when the dogs stirred and ambled over to the door, barking in a desultory fashion. "Come on in," she yelled, assuming the afternoon talk shows were either too boring for words or too scandalous for George. The door opened and shut, and the dogs bounded back into the kitchen.

"You wanted me to sign some papers?"

Kate's head jerked up at Jay's voice. "Oh. I thought you were George." His face was red with cold, and his hair glistened from the mist. He peeled off soaked leather gloves and rubbed his hands over the stove. The uncomfortable silence was broken only by the crackling of burning wood and the dogs' panting. "You see, when Oprah and Geraldo get too scandalous," she started, then stopped. He looked at her questioningly. "Well, George comes over and...he lives alone. You want some coffee?"

"Sounds good. Do you lock your doors at night?"

"The cups are to the right of the sink," she said, scooting closer to the table. "And why would I need locks? I have dogs." Molly sniffed at Jay's jeans and Chester lay flat on his side, his tail thumping.

Jay rubbed Molly's ears and raised an eyebrow at Chester. "Trained to kill, no doubt."

"Well, who needs them," she said, and nodded toward Snit, "when you have an attack cat?" Good Lord, why did he make her so nervous? Probably because she hadn't combed her hair or really bothered to dress this morning. She had on ratty sweats and pink bunny slippers—complete with floppy ears, black noses and whiskers. They were a Christmas gag gift from Mary Beth, but Kate had discovered they kept her feet absolutely toasty on the cold floors of the old farmhouse.

Jay poured a cup of coffee and arched his eyebrows toward the chair across from her. She nodded and shuffled through the papers on the table, hoping she wouldn't have to traipse off to the study to find the necessary forms. She dug out an I-9 that looked as if one of the dogs had slobbered on it and flattened it as best she could. "You fill out the top part and I'll do the rest of it."

He quickly filled in the top, signed it and handed it back to her, along with a social-security card and driver's license. She noted his address in Kenwood, California.

"Whereabouts is Kenwood?" she asked, completing the form.

"Northern."

"Luther Thomas, the new owner of the big farm, is from somewhere near Glen Ellen. Are you familiar with the Thomas Winery?" Jay looked around the kitchen, taking in all the clutter. She wished she'd done a little straightening up.

"I've seen it. Have you had the tractors and sprayers serviced this winter?" he asked harshly.

Kate flinched at his tone. So much for chitchat and dragging any information out of him. "Not yet. I'll get someone to do it before long."

"I'll do it when I can't work outside." He leaned back and sipped his coffee as if forcing himself to relax. "You have quite a fan club among the ladies in the neighborhood."

She squirmed in her chair at the sudden change in his voice. Lord, he was as moody and unpredictable as Snit. "You've done pretty well yourself," she muttered. "You better be careful or they'll have you married off before summer." She stopped when she realized what she'd said.

"Do they have *you* in mind?"

Something flickered in his eyes. Anger, fire, she wasn't sure what, but the intensity of it prickled the back of her neck. "No. I mean, of course not. But they'll find someone," she added in a lame attempt to keep things light.

"Not likely."

The bitterness in his voice made her flinch again, and her curiosity soared another notch. At that moment the kittens thundered down the stairs, sailed over Chester, over the table and out through the cat door on the closed-in back porch, little more than a blur of yellow and gray. Jay tensed and started up, but by then they were gone. Papers fluttered to the floor. "Was that—"

"Apollo and Stagger Lee," she said.

"Apollo and Stagger Lee. The same ones you—" he pulled his jacket away from his chest in an exaggerated fashion "'—carry around?" A smile threatened to come, but disappeared. "You run a shelter on the side?"

"I like animals," she said defensively. Why did she feel so obliged to explain everything to him? She looked up into his unwavering gaze and saw that "something" flicker again, burning a path across everything it touched. Which at that moment happened to be *her*. For some reason breathing became an impossibility.

"If you have the W-4," he said with a note of amusement in his voice, "I'll sign it and get back to work."

She breathed again. "Right. I'll just run find one." She desperately wanted to jump up from the table, get the forms signed and escort him out of her house, but there was the problem of the bunny shoes. Snit chose that moment to spring from the counter to the middle of the table. Papers flew as the cat settled herself in front of Jay and stared at him.

"Hey, puss," he said softly, and offered his hand.

There was something about the gentleness in his voice that made Kate's heart pound a little faster. "The name is Snit," she said, trying to quell these unbidden feelings. "And for very good reasons. You'll probably lose your hand if you don't keep it to yourself. She's a very unreliable cat."

He scratched the cat under the chin, and Snit offered her neck. Kate heard the cat's rumbling purr begin as Jay said she was a lovely lady.

"Yeah, well, if she stops purring and gets a weird look in her eyes, hit the deck."

His finger stroked the cat's neck. "I don't think so."

Kate couldn't believe her infamous attack cat was turning to putty right in the middle of the kitchen table. "People have left this house without their faces. Ask Chester," she said, knowing that Snit was going to make a liar out of her. She watched Jay's fingers, so gentle, so sure, and found herself wondering how they would feel on her neck—which reddened at the thought.

"They don't know how to handle an elegant lady."

Kate gnawed on the pencil, trying to shake off the feelings sweeping over her. For Snit to make up with him, he had to be a wonderful person—or as much of a psychopath as Snit was. Kate fanned herself with the

I-9 form and hoped for the latter. "I don't believe this."

Jay gave the cat a final stroke and stood. "The form?"

"The form." She jumped up and hurried out of the kitchen, hoping he was staring at Snit, instead of her bunny shoes.

Returning quickly, she handed him the W-4. "You don't have to prune on days like this, you know. Bad days are kind of guilt-free goof-off days." He gave her a look that clearly said there were no such things as goof-off days on a farm.

"I'll work in the shed this afternoon." He turned to go, then lingered by the wood stove as if reluctant to leave. "I took a look at the irrigation pump yesterday. It needs a little work."

She nodded. "The pump guy will be here next month."

"I'll take care of it."

She bristled. He was supposed to be pruning the big farm, not messing around in her pump house. "The pump isn't your responsibility."

His eyebrows arched. "But those berries are. And without water..."

"You'll have water," she snapped, shuffling papers, hoping he'd take the hint and leave, but he stood by the stove, rubbing his hands and staring at her.

"You do your own marketing?"

She nodded. "A marketing co-op handles most growers in the area, but we've had the same customers for years, and we like to take care of them."

A frown creased his face. "We? Meaning the new owner?"

"Yeah, we, meaning the new owner," she said, seething at his tone. "In that old refrigerator truck behind the shed, which I'm sure you don't approve of, but which runs like a scared rabbit." She waved her hand in a vague gesture. "Don't worry, everything will get done. It always does."

"It only gets done if somebody makes sure it gets done." His words crackled like a stick of green wood on a hot fire. "I assumed the big farm was my responsibility."

"It is," she said forcing herself to ignore the angry words and burning eyes. "But since I've been through harvest every year for most of my life and you haven't, you'll just have to trust *my* list of priorities." Why was he getting so bent out of shape about whether everything would be ready? *He* wasn't the one who had to stay awake nights worrying about it. "The pump, the tractor and everything else is on my list."

"Fine. I'll still look them over when I have the time."

"Fine. The pruning comes first." As he started out of the kitchen, she followed him, drawn in spite of herself. He turned and let his eyes trail down her ratty sweat suit.

"Nice shoes," he said harshly, and walked out the door.

"Old farmhouses have cold floors," she called after him. She slammed the door, but pulled the curtain aside and watched him walk down the drive, hunched up against the cold drizzle. She couldn't figure out whether to be delighted or angry that he was a take-charge type. It did take a load off her shoulders, but it probably meant he didn't think she knew what she was doing. He wouldn't be the first man to chafe at

taking orders from a woman. But she didn't want him
to be one of those men. She wanted him to... She went
back to her orders, but the figures swam and rear-
ranged themselves against her will. All she could think
about was... Never mind what she was thinking
about.

As she poured coffee she didn't really need, Snit
reached out and snagged her, then jumped to the food
bowl. "I don't feed traitors," Kate said in a stern
voice. "How could you?" The cat sat in front of the
food bowl, looking smug. "You're going to ruin your
reputation, cat."

A FEW MINUTES after Kate ordered a large supreme
with anchovies, Barry came jogging in, pulled her out
of the booth and smothered her in a bear hug. "Would
you believe our illustrious prosecuting attorney just
called off a deal we agreed to a month ago? And it's
not even close to election time. If he thinks I'm going
to fold... A jury will never convict on what he's got."

"So why make a deal in the first place?"

"Well, maybe they wouldn't convict. My client has
a guilty look."

Kate laughed. "The whole system comes down to
looks?"

"Remember Otis Townsend in the sixth grade? Always getting blamed for everything? Well, he had that
expression. Very tough to fight that with a jury."

Kate shook her head. "Poor Otis wouldn't ever
meet your eyes. I wonder what happened to him?"

"Probably in jail for something he didn't do. Ju-
ries much prefer a liar who'll try to stare them down."

"Good Lord, Barry, this all sounds very depress-
ing."

"Not so. It's wonderful." He sighed. "I called the hospital. Angie went off duty at three."

"What happened to Kitty?" Barry always fell in love with women whose names ended in *ie* or *y*.

"Kitty's history. She thinks I'm a workaholic."

"Only because you are."

"In ten years I'll have *the* criminal law firm in this region. Women are supposed to love ambitious men."

"Times are changing, Barry. Women want their men around these days."

He sighed again. "It doesn't matter what you do. It's wrong where women are concerned."

"Hang in there, Barry. Maybe Angie is the one."

The pizza came and Barry tore off a slice. "I hear you have, according to Mary Beth, an absolutely gorgeous hunk working for you. Gladys talked more in terms of lovely."

Kate shook her finger at him. "Barry Wade, you're a worse gossip than Gladys and crew ever thought about being. And he's not working for me— He's working for the new owner."

"One has to keep up with the goings-on in the neighborhood. But back to the hunk— Who is he? Gladys is enchanted."

"He's just a guy I hired to prune, and if he works out he's going to run the place till Mr. Thomas gets here."

"Just a guy?" he said around a mouthful of pizza. "Sounds very suspicious. You know anything about him?"

Kate took a bite and felt the hot cheese sear her tongue. "What's to know? I'm not hiring a CEO or a space engineer. We're not talking high tech."

"What's his name? I'll have a friend of mine in the sheriff's office check him out."

"Don't you dare. He passed muster with Chester, Molly and me." An image of Jay sitting at her table stroking Snit floated through her mind's eye. "And even with Snit," she added softly.

"Snit? This *does* sound serious."

"Barry, I thought we came here to talk about Angie."

"It won't work out. They never do. They can't measure up to you, sweet."

Kate choked on her pizza. "Try somebody whose name doesn't end in *ie* or *y.* "

"What does that have to do with anything?"

"Figure it out." They finished the pizza, then lingered over coffee, talking about mutual friends until Barry, who had a court case the next morning, called it a night.

Kate got home in time to sit by the fire and watch Miss Marple deal with a mysterious rash of anonymous letters in a quiet English village. The kittens played with her slippers, finally crawling into her lap to sleep. Chester and Molly sprawled at her feet and all was right with the world. Almost.

Because there were times, like tonight, when her house and farm and animals weren't quite enough. Times when she wanted more, when she missed something—not missed, exactly, since she'd never had it— when a vague restless yearning stirred deep within her. A yearning for something she didn't even have a name for. "Not something," she murmured, stroking the kittens, "someone." These feelings usually came after an evening with Barry. Barry, who wanted a wife and family so badly he didn't know what to do about it. She kept telling him it would happen if he quit worrying about it, quit chasing it so hard.

But the fact was, they both lived in a very small town, and potential mates were limited. She'd had her chance once, not with Barry, but with a man who... She pushed the thought aside, unwilling to dredge up old memories. Poor Barry. He was still frantic to find his future. Kate had—or so she told herself—made peace with her future.

But the yearning tonight was stronger than before, and no longer vague. It had a name. And a shape. And eyes the color of oak leaves in spring.

CHAPTER FOUR

KATE CUT the cane and threw it as far as she could. Chester and Molly raced after it as if they, too, knew another pruning season was over.

"These rows get longer ever' year," George said with a sigh. "Reckon that boy's ever gonna get finished?" He nodded toward the big farm.

"At the rate he's going he must be working with a flashlight at night."

It was a beautiful day, the sky so clear and blue it hurt your eyes. The long-range forecast was for normal temperatures, but Kate could feel spring gathering, feel the push of buds swelling, ready to burst into bloom. "Going to be an early season, George."

"Mmm. Got to hand it to the boy. He's a hard worker."

That might be the understatement of all time. Jay was obsessed with work—and with staying out of her sight. It was like having a robot on the big farm. He looked like a man, walked like a man, but he worked like a machine. And he talked only when absolutely necessary.

"We'll do the herbicide tomorrow," she said. "These bushes will be blooming before we know it." An early season meant a better crop and better prices, but it also meant that she was never quite ready.

"If I can get outta bed," George quipped.

"Call me. I'll haul you out with the tractor."

It was still early afternoon when she returned to the house. Plenty of time to get the supply orders sent and write to Luther Thomas. Frankly, she was getting a wee bit panicky. Although she didn't want to bother him, she *had* broken down a few nights ago and phoned, only to find herself talking to an answering machine. She left a cheery message that she had hired someone and that everything was under control. And Jay *could* handle the farm, but, there were supplies to order and she had to call the Mexican families in south Texas and make arrangements if Luther wanted them. She had to pay them... She sighed and sat down at the kitchen table to draft a letter that would sound businesslike rather than cheery—or panicky. But thirty-five acres of blueberries required up-front operating capital, and she didn't have that kind of capital—not for her farm *and* the big one. She was deep into the letter when the phone rang. It was Gladys.

"Kate, dear, you've been working yourself to death. Dinner's at six and I won't take no for an answer."

"I have a lot to do, Gladys—"

"Nonsense, you have to eat. Six o'clock. And no, you cannot bring anything."

Kate drove to town, mailed her letters, got a few bare essentials, mostly dog and cat food, and went home to resume her worrying.

"YOO-HOO!" Kate called as she stepped into Gladys's house that evening. Gladys considered it an insult if neighbors knocked.

"In the kitchen."

Kate walked down the narrow hall, breathing in great drafts of warm fried-chicken-laden air. Gravy, mashed potatoes... She sighed. Cholesterol city, but how could anything so good possibly be bad for you? "I'm so hungry I could eat a..." The words died on her lips as she turned the corner and crashed into Jay, who was stirring a steaming skillet of gravy. And who at the moment looked as if he would like to toss the gravy and chew on the iron skillet.

"Oh," Kate said, backing away. "I didn't know..."

"I'll bet," he muttered, and stirred with a vengeance.

"Oh, there you are, dear," Gladys bubbled, waving a pan of hot biscuits. "I'm teaching Jay to make gravy. The poor boy never even heard of milk gravy before he came to Arkansas. Now he can't get enough of it."

"Oh," Kate repeated, trying desperately to think of some reason she couldn't stay to eat. Then Gladys's words seeped into her confusion. *Can't get enough?* That meant Jay had eaten here before. Several times. Had they concocted this little party? She sneaked a look at Jay and decided the steam wreathing his head was coming from his ears rather than the gravy. Which was a pretty clear indicator that *he* hadn't been a conspirator.

"The green tomato pickles are in the fridge," Gladys said, and glanced toward the stove. "Turn the fire out, dear. It'll thicken up by the time everything's on the table. You children are working entirely too hard, and people who live alone *never* eat right."

Gladys's kitchen was small in the best of circumstances, but Kate felt as if it had shrunk by at least half as she tried to get to the refrigerator without touching Jay. The warm moist atmosphere, the smell of food and the cramped quarters all made her feel faint.

"Excuse me," she muttered, and yanked open the refrigerator door, hoping the rush of cold air would revive her.

By the time she had hauled about a ton of food to the dining-room table, Kate was fit to be tied. She couldn't decide whether to kill Gladys for playing Cupid, or Jay for thinking what he was thinking. She could tell by his glare he was convinced she had conned dear sweet Gladys into this cozy little supper. *Do you ever have a lot to learn about Gladys,* she thought, slamming the gravy bowl down on the table. When it came to managing people's lives, Gladys made Machiavelli look like a rank amateur.

Kate snatched a molded salad from Jay and told him to go sit down. He went to the dining room without a word. "I will never forgive you for this, Gladys," she whispered fiercely. "How could you?"

Gladys looked at Kate, a picture of innocence. "Do what, dear? It's just a little supper."

"A little supper? For heaven's sake, there's enough food here to feed Cox's army. You could have at least told me he was coming."

"Don't be silly. You wouldn't have shown your face."

Kate fumed. "You're right. And I'll never come to supper again. Never, ever. Not if I die from starvation. Now sometime during this ordeal, you are going to make it very clear to that man I had nothing to do with this."

Gladys frowned. "Oh, dear. Oh, I see. You think he thinks . . . but he thinks you think . . . of course . . ."

"Never mind. The salad's melting." Gladys's logic was tricky at the best of times. And Kate knew all her ranting and raving went in one ear and out the other.

She marched into the dining room and sat down across from Jay. Gladys chattered and passed endless dishes, of which Jay took enormous amounts and Kate took just enough to avoid a scolding from Gladys. Even the thought of eating made her stomach turn. She was very carefully mixing her potatoes and gravy—anything to kill time—when she became aware of the silence. Looking up, she found herself snared in the smoldering depths of Jay's eyes.

"For heaven's sake, Kate, you're going to wear those potatoes out with all that stirring," Gladys said brightly.

Kate tore her gaze away from Jay and shoveled a forkful of potatoes into her mouth.

"I'll swear," Gladys said, shaking her head. "Jay, this was not Kate's doing. Kate, this was not Jay's doing. Now you two lighten up and eat."

Kate stared at the older woman. "Lighten up? Where on earth did you learn that one?"

"My grandson. Don't you just love it?"

Kate burst out laughing and looked at Jay. Whatever their problem was, it wasn't fair to ruin Gladys's evening. But as soon as their eyes met, she wished they hadn't. He was smiling. Truly smiling. And ...

Jay nodded slightly. "You won't have any leftovers, Gladys."

Laughter had replaced the searing anger in his eyes. Kate began to eat with enthusiasm.

"That's better," Gladys said, beaming. "Children are so touchy these days. Now what's the status of the strawberries, Kate? I'm getting calls from everywhere." Gladys was the strawberry grapevine each year, passing out regular reports to all her friends and relatives.

Kate swallowed a delicious mouthful of biscuit and gravy. "The buds are peeking out of the crowns. We'll put the straw down in a week or so, assuming Howard gets it here."

"You'd best call him and remind him, dear."

"You mulch with straw?" Jay asked.

Kate nodded. "I think they'll be early this year. Maybe the first week in May if the weather holds. We'll no doubt have a few frosts along the way."

"You can't imagine what this child goes through every spring with her strawberries. Up all night, walking the fields in the cold, worrying herself sick."

Jay arched an eyebrow at her. "You don't have temperature sensors on the sprinkler system?"

Kate shrugged. "I like to turn the system on myself."

"I've never understood how you can possibly keep something from freezing by coating it with ice," Gladys sighed. When Jay started to explain, she held up her hand. "Oh, I've heard all about the mysterious heat of fusion, but it still doesn't make a whit of sense to me. I'll get the blueberry cobbler if you'll get the ice cream, Kate."

Kate groaned. "Blueberries? How could you?"

Gladys laughed. "Not everyone is so jaded. Jay needs to know what he's working for."

As Gladys disappeared into the kitchen, Kate jumped up and hurried off to the freezer on the back porch. Even if all the misunderstandings about why they were having dinner together were understood— which she didn't think for a minute they were—the idea of being alone with him made her nervous.

"When are Sarah and Leonard coming back?" Gladys asked as she dished out enormous helpings of cobbler.

"The first of May, I guess," Kate replied, spooning on the ice cream with more restraint. "Daddy's driving Mom crazy taking flying lessons. In an ultralight plane."

Gladys stopped dead in the doorway to the dining room. "*What* is *that?*"

Kate laughed. "According to Mom it's a contraption of flimsy wires and nylon hooked to a lawn chair and powered by a chain-saw motor."

Gladys frowned as she set down two bowls of dessert and Kate followed with the third. "My word, has Leonard lost his mind?"

Kate had asked her mother the same question, then convinced herself that it was probably a passing fancy and her father would come to his senses before he tried to solo—or worse, bought his own ultralight. "Probably. I think he doesn't have his tractors to play with anymore, so he's looking for a new machine to master."

Gladys shook her head. "Falling off a tractor is one thing. Falling out of the sky is quite another. I'll call them tomorrow." Kate smiled, knowing Gladys would give Leonard what-for.

"They're actually quite safe," Jay said quietly.

Both women looked at him.

"They are," he insisted, "if he has a good instructor." When they continued to stare at him, he shrugged. "I've tried ultralights and hang gliders. They're fun."

Gladys snorted. "Leonard's old enough to know better. He'll get over it when he gets back here where he belongs."

Jay looked at Kate, a slight frown creasing his forehead. "I didn't realize your folks were coming back," he said quietly.

Something in his voice stung. "Just to help me out with the harvest," she informed him, and bent to her cobbler. Her answer had eased his frown a bit, but he was still strangely silent. What was it to him if her parents came back?

Half an hour later, during which time Jay seemed to relax again and consume almost half the cobbler, Gladys started carrying things to the kitchen.

"Now you two run along. I'll clean up. I'm sure you have to be out at the crack of dawn doing your chores." The pair had followed her into the kitchen, and now she shooed them out. "Go on, go on."

Kate wasn't about to endure the walk home beside Jay—a walk that would be memorable, no doubt, for its silence. "No, Gladys. I will never come to supper again if you don't let me help. Jay's off the hook this time," she said brightly, "but I'm washing." At which point she made the mistake of looking at Jay and knew from the sly smile he gave her that he clearly understood why she was staying.

"I don't bite," he whispered, "unless the moon is full."

"Cute," she whispered back. "Very cute." It was the first hint of humor she'd seen in the man. So why wasn't she relieved to discover he wasn't all work? His voice had been filled with . . . with . . . It was sexy, that was what it was. She turned on her heel before he could say anything else and hurried back to the kitchen. Gladys trailed behind her.

"Isn't he the sweetest—"

Kate plunged her hands into the hot soapy water. "Don't start, Gladys. Don't you dare even breathe a word to me of what's going on in that devious mind of yours."

"Oh, this is encouraging, dear. I haven't seen you this mad since Barry stole your clothes off the willow bush and I had to haul you home wrapped in my apron. Oh, my, yes, this *is* encouraging."

Kate almost scrubbed the finish off the dishes. She would straighten everything out with Jay in the morning. When she got through he would understand that *she* had been the victim of this dinner, not him. She swiped her forehead with the sleeve of her sweatshirt. "What have you got the thermostat turned to, Gladys? I'm about to burn up."

Gladys's laughter filled the kitchen. "Of course you are, dear. I'll get a fan."

The next morning Kate was fussy, bordering on surly. Her restless sleep had been filled with dreams that weren't dreams, but more in line with the wishful thinking that occurs in that twilight zone between wakefulness and sleep. Dreams about Jay were bad enough, but wishful thinking? Inexcusable. For whatever reason, he was a temporary part of her life, running from something she couldn't even begin to imagine. Not the kind of man to think about in the wee hours of the morning. It wasn't as if he was pursuing her or anything. He hardly spoke to her most days. And then to break his silence with a heart-wrenching smile and "I don't bite..." She didn't think she could stand it. Any of it.

"Talk about dreams made of smoke," she lectured Snit as she dished out cat food. "The stupidest kind of dreams." Snit didn't even bother to sniff the food before she swung at Kate. "Don't push it, Snit. Do you know how much this stupid can of cat food cost? Do you know how long I have to work out in the fields to feed you? Do you know how many cats are starving in China? Or New York? Or wherever?"

The cat ignored her and tried to bury her breakfast. "One of these days, cat, *pow! Kaboom!* No more finicky cat!" After her threats failed to impress Snit, Kate gave the offending food to the kittens and opened a small can of the expensive stuff, just as she always did.

A few minutes later she was on her way to the shed with a mug of coffee. It was a good hour till daylight, but she couldn't hang around the house another minute. She would hook the spray rig to the tractor and calibrate it so George could put down the herbicide this morning. Automatically she checked the weather. Calm, a heavy dew—perfect weather for spraying.

She got the pump mounted on the tractor's power-takeoff shaft with no problem. Got the tank mounted behind the tractor with no problem. Got all of the bolts that attached the spray boom to the tractor off—except for the last one, which defied all her efforts. She tried bigger wrenches, penetrating oil, cussing and yelling. After thirty minutes all she had to show for her efforts was three banged-up knuckles, four streaks of oil on her face and a broken wrench. "It was never this hard when Daddy did it," she railed at the dogs, who quietly retired to a spot under a wagon. "Leverage, that's what I need. More leverage."

Putting the socket on the longest ratchet tool she had, Kate slipped a four-foot piece of iron pipe over the end. She was now six feet from the bolt, and the socket kept slipping off. She got everything in place one more time, put tension on the pipe and lay down across it. When she was sure it wasn't going to come loose and dump her, she put her entire weight on the pipe and began to bounce.

Nothing happened. She bounced harder. Suddenly she was yanked up by the back of her coveralls as if gravity had reversed itself. The rachet and pipe clattered to the concrete floor.

"What are you trying to do? Kill yourself?" Jay set her on her feet and spun her around in one motion.

His eyes were in shadow, but she imagined she saw a flash of concern. "No," she snapped, embarrassed at getting caught in such a silly pose. "I'm trying to loosen that stupid bolt."

"A smashed nose would really add to your looks." Staring at her oily face, his voice softened. "Why didn't you come get me?"

"I don't usually have any trouble." In fact, she'd never hooked up the sprayer by herself.

"Superwoman has to do everything herself," he muttered. "Prove to the world she can do it." He picked up the ratchet, fitted the socket on the bolt and began to exert pressure. "You use penetrating oil?"

"Of course I did. And everything else known to man for loosening bolts, including that gooey hand-cleaner, axle grease and lard." She watched the tendons stand out in his neck and knew that under his sweatshirt, sinewy muscles were bulging with the effort. The bolt finally screamed, then turned.

He ratcheted it off with long easy strokes. "Now, what are you trying to do?"

"I am not *trying* to do anything. I *am* hooking up the spray rig. See that thing over there?" She pointed to a length of pipe, bent into the shape of an upside-down U. "That goes on the tractor. And it's too heavy, because Daddy overbuilds everything. Fortunately hernias don't run in our family."

"I didn't say a word," he said grimly. They picked up the apparatus and fitted it to the tractor, Jay holding it in place while she tightened the bolts. "How do you manage things like this by yourself?" he asked in a taut voice.

"George. Or I call a neighbor. There isn't much I need help with." Although this morning was her first lesson in how many times she *would* now that her father was gone. Still, she wasn't about to admit that to Jay.

"Tough lady," he said softly, more to himself than to her. "You need any help with the spraying?"

She shook her head. "I'll calibrate it, then George can do both farms."

He leaned against the tractor, his arms crossed over his chest, and studied her appraisingly. "You're paying George's time to spray a farm you don't even own?"

She shrugged. "It's a fair trade-off. His equipment, my labor." She started to move around him, but he caught her arm, and when she looked up, a muscle jumped in his jaw.

"The new owner's not here. How's he to know whether you sprayed or not?"

She shook him off. "It doesn't matter whether he knows. *I'd* know." Her eyes flashed with anger. "And don't get any ideas about shortcuts or you're out of here."

He caught her again, this time by the wrist. "You won't get rid of me on that account." His voice was edged with steel.

It was as if a field of energy crackled between them. "I'm not looking to get rid of you," she said in a husky voice. "I'm setting the ground rules."

He stood there, staring at her for a long moment. Finally he let her go and stepped back. "I was surprised, that's all. Honesty is . . . rare."

"Not on this farm," she said quietly, her eyes holding his, searching for something undefinable she'd heard in his voice. The exchange had shaken her. "The only thing worse than a thief is a liar. I won't have either on this farm."

"You don't have to worry on either count."

"Good." She couldn't imagine why, but for a split second she'd sensed a vulnerability about him she didn't even want to think about. And she certainly didn't want to think about the fire lingering in her wrist and burning its way toward her stomach. She started out of the shed for a dose of nice cold morning air. Then she remembered the fiasco at Gladys's. The dogs had ambled out from under the wagon, and she reached down to fondle Chester's ears. "About last night . . ." she started.

Jay squatted and let Molly lick his face. "Forget it."

"I didn't know . . . I mean, it wasn't my idea. What I mean is, Gladys is notorious for organizing people's lives." She glanced at him. He was wrestling with Molly's enormous head, but his eyes never left hers. "You have to—"

"Maybe we could eat out some evening in town and you can tell me what the harvest's like."

"I assure you it won't happen again," she persevered. "I wouldn't dream of putting you in a position..." Her voice trailed off and her pulse rate jumped a notch. "Do what?"

"Go out to eat."

"Oh. But I was just explaining..." She was burning up again. She wiped her face with her sleeve and managed to rearrange the streaks of oil into huge smears.

"Without Gladys."

"Without Gladys. Right." Kate searched for all the reasons she couldn't possibly have dinner with this man. Bad precedent, fraternizing, nothing to wear...

He cleared his throat. "It's not a date or anything. Just a chance to talk about the farm."

Kate sighed. "Of course not. Not a date or anything."

"Maybe a burger or something. Give me some idea of what I'm facing for the next few months."

"Right. A burger or something." Kate's heart was beating at marathon speed.

"Or don't you go out with the hired hands?" His voice suddenly had a sharp edge.

"No. Yes. I mean none of them ever asked. Do you like thick burgers? With real homemade fries?" He smiled, really smiled, and Kate thought she might faint dead away.

"Yeah," he said softly, "I haven't had any real fries in a long time."

"Well, okay. Uh, whenever is good for you." She sailed out of the shed, gulping in the fresh air and thinking with every step that she was forgetting something.

"Haven't you forgotten something?" Jay called.

She turned around and went back. "What?"

"You were going to calibrate the sprayer."

"Right now. I'm going to do that right now."

He nodded toward the John Deere. "Don't you need the tractor?"

Kate felt herself turn red. Good Lord, he must think she was a brainless twit. "The tractor. Right." She hurried to the tractor and started it—before he could say another word to her, before he could make her feel any more like a teenager than she already felt. Fortunately he opened the wide sliding doors. Given her present dither, she probably would have driven right through the side of the shed. "Get a grip," she muttered as she trundled the tractor and its unwieldy rig out into the morning.

CHAPTER FIVE

THREE DAYS LATER, Kate and the kittens were trying to decide what she should wear on a date that wasn't a date. More precisely, *she* was standing in front of the closet while the kittens dangled precariously on the clothes, attempting to work their way up to the blanket shelf.

"It's a good thing my closet is full of cotton, instead of silk," she said, extracting their needle-sharp claws and setting them up on the shelf, where they mewed in disappointment. They were at that gangly stage now, all ears and legs, neither kitten nor cat. Within minutes they managed to dislodge a stack of blankets, and kittens and blankets tumbled to the floor. Kate laughed at their bewilderment. "That was fun, wasn't it? Why don't you go chase Chester?"

In the end, she put on a pair of navy slacks and the burgundy sweater that Mary Beth said brought out the violet in her eyes. She fed everybody, then sat down to watch the TV news and wait—and wonder if she was doing the right thing. She could write up a work schedule and hand it to Jay some morning. Or invite him for coffee and tell him what lay ahead. She could do any number of things besides go out to eat, even if it was only burgers. Except deep down she wanted to go, wanted to get to know him, wanted... "Good heavens," she railed at the kittens. "You'd think I'd never been out to eat with a man." And the truth was, if she didn't count Barry, she hadn't, not for a long long time.

She'd carefully locked away all her romantic yearnings. Locked them away years ago when she broke off an engagement to a man who had wanted the same things she did—land, a way of life. He'd started working for Leonard in the fall. The pruning had gone fine. The spraying had gone fine. The harvest had turned into a nightmare. A late freeze, heavy rains, labor problems. The second week into the harvest, Toby had come apart like a dollar watch and stormed off the farm, yelling that people who thought they could make a living off bushes ought to have their heads examined.

He'd called a week later to beg Kate to go to Oklahoma with him—to his dad's cattle ranch. Toby had suddenly fallen in love with all those cows he'd spent his childhood hating. "It's not grunt work," he'd said.

She'd often thought if it had been an easier season, if she hadn't already bought the old farmhouse from her parents, hadn't planted her first berries, if... She swallowed hard. Those memories hadn't seen daylight in years, but she hadn't forgotten them.

Toby had started something he didn't finish, which was a cardinal sin where a Harmon was concerned. It had to do with respect and a man's word. She wasn't sure she *could* have given up green mountains for the flat prairies of Oklahoma, given up the smell of fresh-turned earth in the spring and the first bud break for a four-legged crop. But she damn sure couldn't give it up for a man she no longer respected.

She didn't date much after Toby, so there had been no one to ask her to sacrifice a huge chunk of who she was. And no one to whom she was willing to offer that much.

When Jay knocked, she almost jumped out of her skin, and when she opened the door, the greeting she had carefully planned—a brief description of how to check irrigation drip lines—froze in her throat. Pale gray slacks, instead of jeans, a moss-green shirt, a leather jacket so soft she wanted to touch it, his hair curling and still damp, the sharp delicious smell of something foresty and wild...

She had no idea how long she stood and stared. "We need to check the drip system soon," she croaked at last. He smiled, which didn't help matters at all.

"You do have a way with small talk. Ready?"

"Ready." She knew she should get a jacket, but abandoned the idea. For some reason, she seemed to be burning up again.

He scrutinized her closely—from head to toe—and his eyebrows arched as he gave an approving nod. "A real improvement over an insulated coverall."

Kate flew out of the house and jumped in the Bronco before he could open the door—in the unlikely event he was going to do so. There was a moment, after his left-handed compliment, that she could have sworn he was about to take her arm. Certainly whatever she'd seen in those gorgeous eyes wasn't his usual mad-at-the-world look. She sighed and thought maybe mad was easier to deal with than nice. Mad didn't make her nearly so warm.

As Jay pulled onto the county road, he said seriously, "Now, about the drip system."

She rolled down the window, took a couple of deep breaths and launched into a lengthy explanation of everything she knew about irrigation. By the time they got to Fayetteville, she felt better and directed Jay to the D-Lux burger place near the university.

When they were seated, however, and Jay peeled off his jacket, her control wavered and thoughts of irrigation fled. She ordered a beer and tried not to wonder if his chest was as bronze as his arms.

Amusement flickered in his eyes. "You look a little flushed."

Why was he suddenly being so damned charming? "I'm fine." She took a long swallow of cold beer and lectured herself severely on acting her age. "So how do you like blueberries so far?"

He shrugged. "So far, okay. They're very different from grapes."

"We almost put in some table grapes a few years ago, but the spray schedule! Every fungus and bug in the world is sitting out there waiting for grapes."

He laughed. "This humid climate would be a problem. They like plenty of water underground and a desert above. What's the spray schedule for the blues?"

"Very little, which I like. Every few years you have bud borer, occasionally inch worms, and if you have hail damage, you hit them with a fungicide just to be safe." Kate felt better now that they were back on farm matters.

The food came and Jay examined a steaming fry. "These potatoes have never seen a freezer bag." He bit the end and groaned. "Ah, memories of the drive-in when I was in high school." He reached for another. "So what do you do when you're not farming?"

She took a bite of her burger, unsure how to answer. "There's always something to do on a farm," she finally said, wiping her mouth. It was impossible to eat a D-Lux burger without dripping shamelessly.

He studied her, his eyebrows raised. "Surely you do something for fun. Shop, travel... something."

She looked at him in surprise. "What I do *is* fun." When he frowned, she rushed on to explain, which she'd become accustomed to doing over the years. "I mean, it's not always fun. It's hard work and any job where you depend on the weather is risky, but..." Why did she always have to justify her life-style to everyone? Nurses didn't have to. Teachers didn't have to. She quickly drained her glass, then wished she hadn't. "I can't imagine doing anything else."

"No husband in your future?" He leaned forward, his eyes capturing hers. "No kids to carry on? Just the farm? Forever?"

Kate felt a bit dizzy since she wasn't much of a beer drinker—but not dizzy enough to miss the mockery in his voice. She leaned closer and glared at him. "Yeah. Just the farm. Now, do you want to talk about the summer schedule or not?"

He sat back, smiling. "I didn't mean to touch a sore spot."

"It's not a sore spot, but I get tired of defending my life to everybody. Have I asked you what you're doing on a blueberry farm in Arkansas when it's obvious you could be making a lot more money doing any number of other things?" She was pleased to see him shift uncomfortably in his seat.

"We weren't talking about me."

A vein popped up at his temple and she smiled. "Sore spot?"

"No," he muttered. He took a bite of his burger. "Maybe we should stick to farm matters."

"Maybe we should," she said, and popped a fry in her mouth.

He signaled the waitress for two more beers. "So what am I looking at for the next couple of months?"

Kate breathed easier. "The irrigation system first, then we get the equipment ready. Packing tables and lines, field flats, buckets, all that sort of thing."

When Kate finally looked at her watch it was two hours later. They had talked blueberries, strawberries, grapes, then somehow, he had cleverly drawn her into rattling on about pets, college, a little of everything. And while she hadn't learned one bit more about his mysterious life, she knew more about *him*. The love for growing things burned just as brightly in Jay as it did in her. Which, when she thought about it, made another sort of fire flame deep within her. Before she could think about the disaster inherent in that, they were on their way to the car and she was telling him what a wonderful time she'd had.

The cold air sobered her. After all, one doesn't have a wonderful time with one's farm manager, especially when he really isn't one's farm manager. "I didn't mean I had a *wonderful* time. I mean, it's nice to talk to someone who knows about the same things."

He put his arm around her shoulders. "Hey, *I* had a wonderful time. I haven't had a burger and fries like that since college. Now if I had a magic potion that would settle all that food..."

Shivering, she leaned against him, savoring the warmth of his body, forgetting for the moment where she was—and who she was snuggled against. Her arm circled his waist as if it belonged there. "A cherry limeade is the very thing for neutralizing junk food," she said, laughing.

"Cherry limeade?"

"Absolutely. There was one drugstore that still had a soda fountain when I was a kid. Any time I had a stomachache, Mom would drive in and bring me a cherry limeade. The soda fountain closed," she said as they reached the Bronco, "but I have all the makings at home."

Jay reached for the door, then stopped to tuck a strand of hair behind her ear. "You are an absolute wealth of strange and wonderful information."

When her back touched the Bronco, the metallic cold seeped through her sweater and swept away any lingering effects of the beer. Jay's face was inches from hers, his eyes flickering with something that couldn't possibly be there. She shivered again, not from the cold, but from his touch.

"You want my jacket?" he said softly.

"No. I think..." She reached for the door handle to quell the sudden physical response that started deep inside and radiated out like the swirling heat of a brushfire on a wintry day—strange and exciting and scary. The kind of feelings dreams are made of. "I guess we should get moving," she murmured, desperate to put some distance between them, distance enough for her to look at those feelings without being overwhelmed by them.

"It's not even eight o'clock," he said, stroking her cheek. "Afraid the farm will run off while we're gone?"

Her breathing turned ragged and alarm bells clanged. "Why are you doing this?" she whispered, attempting to regain some control.

"You don't like it?" He touched the pounding pulse in her throat. "I think you do."

She brushed his hand away. "You hardly speak for days at a time, then for no good reason you turn into Prince Charming. Why?" His face grew rigid, but his eyes burned.

"I'm trying to make up my mind about you."

"About what?" she said, struggling to maintain her composure. "And what am I supposed to do in the meantime? Be friendly? Ignore you? Send you a note every morning to ask about your mood before I speak? I take that from Snit, but not from human beings." She was pushing it, but she had to know if this was real—or a game. If it was a game, she had to stop it. Now. The stakes were too high.

He leaned against the car behind him. "I just want to get to know you."

"There's nothing to know. This is it." He didn't respond, but the tension in his body was palpable. "And I think you were right the first time. You're trying to make up your mind about something," she said softly, "but I don't think it has a damn thing to do with me." She opened the door, but before she could climb in he took her shoulders, swinging her around to face him.

"You're wrong, Kate," he whispered. "It has everything to do with you." He leaned down until his face was inches from hers. "And you feel it, too. What's the harm in indulging ourselves a little?"

She wrenched out of his grip. "If you don't know the answer to that," she snapped, scrambling into the seat, "you...you... Oh, forget it. And stick to farm business from now on."

"You're right," He slammed the door. "Farm business it is." He walked around the Bronco muttering something about women and being out of his mind.

She sat bolt upright as he maneuvered out of the parking lot. She couldn't believe what had just happened. She'd been ready to fall into his arms without another thought. She'd wanted... *Good grief, what are you thinking of?* Well, she'd taken care of that with her outburst. Good riddance, right? Right!

Jay drove her home in silence, his hands white-knuckled on the steering wheel. He looked like a beautiful statue, stone hard and marble cold.

When he pulled into her drive, she muttered a thanks for the supper and got out. He nodded and spun gravel in his hurry to leave.

Once in the house, she petted everybody, gave the dogs cookies and fed Snit. "Everybody else hires farm managers who end up being drunks or goof-offs, incompetents or just plain weird," she said to the cat. "Me? I end up with the Hunk of the Month. I can't fire him— He's too good. Obviously I'm incapable of carrying on a conversation with a man unless it's about plants or irrigation systems or something equally fascinating. And I'm certainly incapable of a simple good-night kiss." Snit sniffed the food and yowled. "Shut up." Kate sighed. "I can't stand it. I can't stand the thought of going through the entire season working with someone who makes my stomach hurt."

She fixed a tall cherry limeade and drank it down without tasting it. She turned on the television, hoping for a grade-B horror flick. She got Bogart and Bacall. She turned it off. She tried to analyze her feelings, as if by dragging them out into the open she could make them go away. Which of course brought up the question, *Do you want them to go away?* "Of course I do," she informed Apollo when he climbed onto her lap. She was well into that line of reasoning when the phone rang.

"Don't tell me you've been out on the town," Barry greeted her. "Maybe with your farm manager?"

"What is it, Barry? Has Angie run off with a dermatologist?"

"My, but we're testy tonight."

"We're tired tonight." She sighed and mentally shifted gears. "So how's the glitzy world of crime?"

"Slow. Gladys tells me you're working yourself to death as usual. Now are you going to tell me what's going on with you and this Jay person, or do I have to come see for myself?"

"Nothing. Wishful thinking on the part of Gladys."

"Mary Beth told—"

"Good night, Barry," Kate said sweetly, and hung up, vowing to kill Gladys *and* Mary Beth at the first opportunity.

"YOO-HOO, KATIE."

The sound of Howard Luff's voice brought Kate out of her nap like a shot. You couldn't conjure up a voice like Howard's in your worst nightmare. She hurried downstairs, knowing a load of straw waited. "I thought you didn't work on Sunday, Howard," she said when she opened the door.

"Shoot, Katie, it might rain and it was either me wrestlin' around tryin' to cover this load up or let you worry about it." He grinned. "You're young. You can stand more worry than me."

"Right. Except there's no rain in the forecast." Which didn't impress Howard at all. "Hang on a minute and let me get some gloves." And call George to see if he could come help. But of course George wasn't home. Sunday was his visiting day. She quickly changed into jeans and work boots and grabbed some leather gloves. When she got outside, Howard was in his truck. The four hundred bales of Kansas wheat straw looked like a castle of gold in the afternoon sun. Kate groaned.

Howard spit a stream of tobacco juice across the drive. "Same place?" Howard Luff was a wiry old man who could have been anywhere from fifty to seventy-five, although the neighborhood consensus was toward the latter. He had hauled hay and straw for almost as long as anyone could remember. And the unloading logistics never failed. If she had a crew lined up, Howard brought half a dozen of his sons and nephews. If she didn't have any help, he came alone. Except always before, her father had been there.

"Same place. I'll get some hay hooks and see if I can rustle up another strong back." She grabbed the hay hooks on her way to Jay's trailer. She hated to bother him, but bothering him was better than killing herself. And besides, everything had been fine since their burger night. He hadn't mentioned it, and she hadn't mentioned it. He'd been grim and preoccupied and not asked questions. She'd stayed busy—and grim—and not asked questions. He'd been in obsessive work mode, instead of hunk mode, and she'd been in farmer mode, instead of twit mode, so everything was just dandy—as long as she didn't dwell on her dreams too much or on the nagging suspicion that she was beginning to like Jay Thomas a whole lot, in spite of her great intentions.

She breathed easier when she saw Jay's Bronco parked beside the trailer. The afternoon was warm, and he had all the trailer windows open. She could hear the television—except when she got closer, she realized it wasn't the television. Jay was on the phone.

"...don't know yet where I'll be," Jay was saying.

Kate stopped. She didn't want to interrupt him, but she didn't want to eavesdrop. She walked slowly toward the door.

"Yeah, I'm a lot better." Jay's voice floated through the open window. "I haven't hit anybody, I even smile once in a while... I'm eating just fine. A wonderful old lady has taken me under her wing. She cooks like an angel, although I'll probably die of cholesterol overload." Smiling at his description of Gladys, Kate raised her hand to knock, then froze at the sound of Jay's laughter.

"No, love, she's seventy if she's a day. I plan to stick with old ladies from now on. They're safe and they're great cooks."

Kate couldn't see his face, but the bitter edge in his words stung her. She took a deep breath and hammered on the door. She heard him say he had to run, heard him say, "Love you, see you in June," before the door opened.

"Could you help us unload the straw?" Kate asked, her mind busy with his last words. June? June was peak season. Was he planning to just up and leave one fine morning in the middle of harvest? she wondered. *Of course he'll up and leave. Before, during or after harvest. Just like Toby did. What's to hold him? You? You as much as told him to buzz off the other night.*

He stood in the open door for a long moment, frowning. "Of course," he said finally.

She handed him a hay hook, angry with herself for getting upset over the possibility of his leaving so soon.

But there was the harvest to think about, after all. It wasn't as if she was interested in him personally. *Right, Katie. And if you believe that, I've got a bridge I'd like to sell you.* "I'm sorry to disturb your Sunday afternoon."

"It's okay."

"I'll help *you* unload the supplies for the big farm." Hopping off the wooden stoop, she started down the drive. "That ought to be a fair trade-off."

He caught up to her and touched her arm. "I'm glad to help. Kate..." he began, but she kept walking.

Howard's truck sat at the edge of the strawberry field with Howard perched on the straw as if he planned to spend the day there. As soon as he saw Kate and Jay, however, he started tossing bales to the ground. She introduced the men, then threw herself into the work, bucking bales into place, making neat rows on the ground that would end up the same size and shape as the load on the truck. "Look," Jay said when they had unloaded about a quarter of the straw, "Howard and I can take care of this."

She buried her hook in a bale, bucked it up to the stack and felt her back muscles protest. "I do this every year." Of course, most years she had more help. But she might as well get used to doing things for herself.

Within half an hour, she and Jay were standing on their own four-bale-high stack. Jay had stripped off his shirt and she was trying hard not to notice the ripple of muscles under bronzed skin every time he picked up a bale.

By the time the truck was almost empty, she was hot, sweaty and had itchy straw in her hair, inside her shirt, everywhere. Her muscles were screaming *stop,* and she knew she wouldn't be able to get out of bed the next morning. She'd be damned if she would let Jay know that.

"Yoo-hoo!" came from the other side of the truck, and Kate could have kissed Gladys for showing up. It saved her the embarrassment of collapsing in front of Howard and Jay.

"Over here, Gladys," she called, wiping her face on her shirtsleeve.

Gladys bustled around the truck and squinted up at them. "Well, I never." She shook a finger at Howard. "Howard Luff, you ought to be horsewhipped letting Kate work like a plow mule. Where are all those boys of yours?"

Howard withered under Gladys's assault. "Off fishin', I reckon. And you know Katie don't listen to anybody."

Gladys turned her wrath on Jay. "And you! Eat my fried chicken, sit at my table and behind my back act like any other old redneck. I'm ashamed of you, young man."

"Yes ma'am," was all Jay could manage. "I told her—"

"You have to be very firm with a Harmon."

"Gladys," Kate protested.

"You come down from there this instant, Katherine Ann Harmon. And—" she waved at the men "—I will deal with you two later."

"Aw, Gladys," Howard protested.

Kate scrambled off the stack, knowing that if she didn't things would get worse—Gladys would go for reinforcements. "I'll be back with your check, Howard," she called over her shoulder as she herded Gladys toward the house.

"The very idea, Kate," the old woman said.

"Did you need something, Gladys? Blueberries? Sugar?"

Gladys laughed. "Well, someone has to look after you with Sarah and Leonard gone. My, my, that boy is a handsome creature, isn't he? Are you making any headway with him? You know, dear, I think someone has hurt him badly. He's so... tense about life."

Which meant he wasn't answering the ten million questions Gladys put to him. Kate was surprised he kept going there, but considering the way Gladys cooked, maybe the interrogations were worth it.

"Well," Gladys continued, "what do *you* think?"

"I hardly notice him."

Gladys laughed. "*I* notice him and I'm seventy years old. You two would have gorgeous children. Could you spare me a quart of frozen berries? The ladies in my church circle said they wouldn't let me in Tuesday if I didn't bring a cobbler. I tried to explain..."

Kate wondered what Gladys did with all those berries. Not that she cared, but sometimes she thought Gladys must be cooking for half the world. "How about a gallon? Then you can make a really big cobbler."

"You're such a dear. I'm very careful to ration my berries so they last exactly until harvest. But that dear boy does love cobbler." She smiled at Kate's quizzical look. "Jay. Well, he needs to keep up his strength."

"What, do you feed him every night?"

"Of course not. But you can't expect a man to work in the fields all day, then go back to the kitchen and cook."

"Well, I do. And I doubt he'd starve."

"Oh, but it's so wonderful to cook for a hearty eater again. You know very well I'd cook for you, but you're so determined to do everything for yourself."

"I know." Kate got a sack of berries, hustling Gladys off before she could resume her lecture to the men. She quickly made out a check and hurried back to the truck, relieved that they were down to the last few bales. Howard spit out his tobacco and said he would see her next year.

Kate looked at the enormous stack of straw. If only it was spread on the field. But that was another day's work.

"You want to cover it?" Jay asked.

"Maybe tomorrow."

He nodded and shrugged on his shirt—for which she was grateful. She wanted him to leave so she could go submerge her battered body in a hot bath. Instead, he picked up her hands. Angry red streaks creased her palms from the wire-tied bales, and her knuckles were swollen and stiff, despite the leather gloves.

He rubbed the red streaks gently with his thumbs. "You don't have to prove anything to me," he said quietly.

She stared at the gentle motion of his thumbs and wondered why she could feel it throughout her entire body. "I'm not. I unload straw every year." His angry preoccupation of recent days seemed to have fled, replaced by... what? She wasn't sure, but she sensed it was dangerous—for her, at any rate.

He shook his head. "Howard says you always *help*. Today you were trying to do it all by yourself."

She pulled away. "I don't know what you're talking about."

"I think you do." Placing his finger under her chin, he lifted her head until she had to look at him. "I could take you out for dinner."

His eyes burned with something she had no name for. "I . . . I'm tired. Maybe some other time."

He held his hands up in surrender. "Okay," he said softly. "Only farm business, right?"

Thirty minutes later, Kate was submerged up to her chin in hot water liberally dosed with bubble bath and horse liniment, hoping it wasn't some sort of fatal combination. Apollo and Stagger Lee sat on the edge of the tub batting at the bubbles.

As the heat seeped into her tired body, she wondered what on earth she was going to do about Jay. There was little doubt he found her attractive, although she sensed that most of the time he fought that attraction. But he would probably take her into his bed for a brief fling if she gave the slightest indication that she was interested. And she was interested. But not in a fling, a way to pass the time. He'd told whoever was on the phone he would see her—at least Kate suspected it was a her—in June, which could only mean he was leaving for good. Nothing else made sense. You didn't up and take a vacation from a farm right in the middle of harvest.

He'd also said that he was only interested in old ladies who could cook. "Eliminates me on both counts," Kate muttered.

She ran through her logic a second time, trying to distance herself. A man like Jay could have his pick of women—probably had known more women than she could begin to imagine. His interest in her could only be transient, and that wasn't good enough. He would be too easy to love and it would hurt too much when he left. Yes, her logic was sound. So why did she feel an ache so deep the hot water and liniment didn't begin to soothe it?

CHAPTER SIX

"COME IN," Kate yelled, lacking the energy to walk to the door. "George saw the straw," she informed the dogs, "and wants to know why I didn't call, then he'll chew out Howard next time he sees him at the feed store, just like he did last year." She poured dog food into two bowls, adding some scraps of chicken she'd been saving. "Howard didn't let me know he was coming," she said to the approaching footsteps.

She looked up when the smell of something delicious hit her. It came from two covered aluminum pie plates that Jay was carrying. "Oh," she said, "you're not . . ."

"Gladys sent you some care packages. She thought you'd be too tired to cook."

Kate set the dogs' dishes on opposite sides of the kitchen, groaning when she straightened up. "Perceptive lady," she said as Jay opened cabinet doors until he found the plates.

"Don't bother," she protested, taking note of his fresh clothes and clean-shaven face. "I'd just as soon eat off the pie plates."

"Where do you keep the coffee?"

"I don't want any coffee."

"Well, I do," he said, opening more cabinet doors. "And sit down before you fall down."

She wasn't the least bit hungry, but it all smelled so good. She ripped off the plastic wrap and discovered smothered steak, mashed potatoes, broccoli, hot rolls and a piece of rhubarb pie. "Mmm. I've been trying for years to figure out how that woman makes onion gravy. She tells me, she shows me, but mine still tastes like dog-food gravy." She put a succulent piece of steak into her mouth and groaned.

Jay sat across the table watching her. "I didn't know they still made flannel nightgowns."

"Mmm," she said around a mouthful of yeasty roll slathered in butter. "You can't possibly live in an old farmhouse without one." She had a forkful of broccoli halfway to her mouth when she realized it was *her* flannel nightgown he was talking about. She looked down, up at him, then at her broccoli. "Oh. I..." She started to rise, but he stopped her with a hand on her arm.

"Don't. It's nice."

She felt the familiar heat of his touch. "But..."

"You're covered from neck to feet," he said softly.

"Right. But..."

"Eat your broccoli."

The vegetable suddenly tasted like straw. She pushed her plate aside, all too aware of his eyes on her.

"I'll get you some coffee to go with the pie."

He set a steaming mug down on the table, then stood behind her, his hand on her shoulder. She winced.

"Stiff?"

"No, not at all." She winced again as his hand started to knead the sore muscles of her shoulder. Before she could object too strenuously, he'd set his own mug on the table and started kneading her other shoulder. "Mmm," she groaned as he hit the right spot.

"Not at all?" he asked, his voice as soft as the first morning light. "Your muscles feel like sacks of ball bearings."

Kate told herself to get up. Or brush his hands away. Or order him to stop. But it felt so good, and gradually she let herself relax. A velvety warmth spread across her shoulders and she leaned into the magical hands that slid from her shoulders to the long muscles of her back, kneading, rubbing, spreading the warmth, coaxing the soreness and knots out. "Where did you learn to do this?" she murmured.

"I was a trainer for the football team in college. I can have you back on the line tomorrow, guaranteed."

He raised her arm and started doing funny things to her upper arm with his fingertips. Not rubbing exactly, not pounding exactly. Squiggling, maybe. Incredible.

"I could do a better job if you were lying flat on the floor," he whispered close to her ear.

"Can't," she said dreamily. "Dogs go crazy. They lick me and walk on me."

"The couch." He gently pulled her to her feet, his hands still working their magic on her back. "Come on."

"Same problem," she said. "Wet noses in my ear."

He led her out of the kitchen. "The bed, then."

She was so relaxed she felt like a rag doll. "Bed. Good idea." As she lifted her foot to the first step, the words sunk in. She stiffened and wriggled away from him. "What do you think you're doing?" she demanded, shaking off her lethargy.

He leaned against the wall and smiled. "I'm trying to make sure you can get out of bed in the morning."

But she saw the familiar fire in the green depths of his eyes, felt her own familiar response. "I suppose you were planning to stay here all night and bodily haul me out in the morning?"

"No," he replied, a lazy smile playing on his face. "But it's not a bad idea."

"It's an awful idea." Even as she said the words, a traitorous thought popped into her mind that it was, in fact, a splendid idea. And her equally traitorous body was clamoring that it was a *magnificent* idea. She backed up the stairs, but she was still too close to him. "I'm fine. Thanks for the supper. Thanks for the massage. Good night."

He folded his arms across his chest. "I didn't have anything in mind other than making you feel better, Katherine Ann." The smile still played on his lips, but his voice held a hard edge.

But if she felt any better, she'd be in trouble. And if he didn't go away she was going to throw herself at him and feel ... Oh, my, what she would feel! "Nobody calls me that except my mother and Gladys. When they're mad."

"It's a beautiful name."

She started up the stairs again, but his hand blocked her way. The intensity of his gaze caught and held her.

"Why isn't there a man up there waiting for you, Kate?"

His stinging words brought her back to reality—and anger. "Maybe the same reason there isn't a woman waiting at that trailer for you. Farmers aren't exactly at the top of the list when it comes to romantic professions," she said. "Particularly get-dirty farming."

"There's nothing wrong with getting dirty."

"I didn't say there was, but if the lack of a man up there doesn't bother me, it damn sure shouldn't bother you." She wanted to strike out, push past him, demand to know why he was leaving in June, but she was caught in his eyes, like a leaf swirling in the lazy current of a summer river.

"Are all the men in Arkansas fools?" He touched her cheek. "Or am I so blind I can't see the flaw?"

She shook her head, not trusting herself to speak. There was only the touch of his finger on her cheek—and his eyes. "What are you talking about now?"

"So innocent, so honest, so up-front. It can't be that simple, Kate Harmon. There's something I'm not seeing." He leaned closer, his fingers tracing intricate patterns on her throat. "We're both adults. I see your feelings in your eyes. Feel them in the pulse here."

"No," she said, and heard the lack of conviction. "It's a bad idea. It's—" His lips brushed hers and she felt as if the sun had reached down and touched her. His kiss was a question, and she answered with a question of her own. She put her hand on his heart, felt the warm strong beat, felt his sharp intake of breath. He cupped the back of her neck, drew her closer and kissed her. Kate returned the kiss with all the passion she had stored away for years. The sudden rush of feelings was exhilarating—and terrifying.

She pulled back to catch her breath, to search his face, for what she couldn't say. "No." Her voice was trembling. "You're leaving—" Her words were lost in another long searing kiss that ended with his sigh.

"Don't say anything, Kate. You're right. It's a bad idea."

But his eyes refuted his words. She saw the desire, the need, swirling there, and saw something else, a fear that was his own or a reflection of hers. But he'd felt the same river of fire flow through, over, between them, and she knew he was fighting for control.

"I don't want this," he said more to himself than to her as he backed down the stairs, his eyes holding hers as if he could freeze her forever on the stairs. "I'll only hurt you. I... I'll see you in the morning." And he was gone.

Kate stood on the steps, unable to move, unwilling to break the spell that enveloped her like a cocoon of silk. At that last moment she would have gone with him, up the stairs to the old brass bed spread with the bright colors of her mother's wedding-ring quilt.

She slid down the wall and sat on the step, her face in her hands. Molly padded up the stairs and lay her head on her lap. "Oh, Molly, what am I going to do?" The dog whined and nuzzled her. "He'll be gone in a month, two months. Back to whatever he ran away from." And she would be left with an ache that even her beloved farm couldn't soothe. Sitting on the stairs with Molly's head in her lap, Kate knew she had to stay away from Jay Thomas.

Which she did for two weeks, working until she dropped. She and George spread the straw on the strawberry fields, raking it until the fields were a sea of gold striped with the greening plants. Jay didn't offer to help, and she didn't ask. She spoke to him only when necessary, and he worked as if driven by the devil. His end of their rare exchanges consisted of nods and grunts and one-word answers. But Kate felt his eyes, burning hot with desire but also with an anger she couldn't begin to comprehend.

The days grew longer; snow-white blossoms appeared in the strawberry field, the blueberry buds swelled, ready to open. The world was awakening to another growing and fruiting season, Kate's favorite time of year. Except this year it was different. Her thoughts were consumed not with the awakening earth, but with the feelings Jay had awakened in her. Feelings she hadn't dared to dream of in years.

"Gonna freeze tonight, missy," George said, looking at the sky. "Sure as God made little green apples."

They were getting the sales stand clean and ready for the strawberry season. "Maybe it'll stay cloudy."

"Supposed to clear up. You want me tonight?"

"No. I'll set the temperature alarm for thirty-three." At one degree above freezing she would begin walking the field, checking thermometers at the low points, watching for the first ice crystals to form. If that happened, she'd turn on the sprinkler system. The water would freeze as it hit the plants, coating each tender blossom in a shimmering mantle of protection. Kate, unlike Gladys, understood the physics of the process, yet after all these years it still seemed like magic. But it did mean long nerve-racking nights.

By midafternoon, the clouds had sailed south on a brisk north wind. Kate went to bed, hoping to catch some sleep in case she was up all night, which seemed likely. She woke at six to the unmistakable sounds of Gladys rummaging in the kitchen and stumbled down the stairs.

"I brought supper, some fruit and a chocolate cake. Chocolate keeps me awake for days if I eat it late at night. It *is* going to freeze tonight, isn't it?"

"I think so. The weather channel's predicting the twenties." Kate peeled a banana and took a bite. "Good grief, there's enough food here to feed an army, Gladys."

"Well, it may have to keep you going for several nights." She frowned at Kate. "You look peaked," she said, drawing out the word until it sounded like a terminal disease. "I swear, I don't know who's sicklier these days, you or that boy."

Kate wiped the surprise off her face. "I'm fine."

"Fine, my foot. You look like a calf that's been in the molasses barrel. And Jay's hardly eating enough to keep a bird alive. What in the world have you done to him?"

Kate stared at the older woman. "What have *I* done to *him?* I haven't done anything to him, and he hasn't done anything to me and—"

"Well," Gladys said, "there you are."

Kate waved her banana. "What's that supposed to mean?"

Gladys caught her arm and examined the banana. "A bruise. They must throw them around like pieces of wood."

"Never mind the banana, Gladys. Jay Thomas is a...a hired hand. Period. He works for Luther Thomas. He's very good at what he does, but he's just killing time here. For what reasons, I have no earthly idea. He's moody. He's closemouthed. He obviously doesn't belong here. He's—"

"A lovely creature, my dear, who needs a little TLC. My word, Kate, you're so good with plants."

Kate didn't want to think about Jay—or about Gladys's not-so-subtle implications. "Oh, nuts. Plants and men are hardly in the same category, Gladys."

"I can't think why not. Now, I've lined up my grandsons if this cold spell drags on. Charles works second shift, so he can spell you at midnight. Randall's laid off, so he can spell you anytime. Just call me."

Kate hugged her. "Thanks, but I think I can handle it. And thanks for all the food."

She put the various dishes in the refrigerator. This was an exciting time of the year for her neighbors. They had all raised strawberries back in the forties or picked them in their childhood, and the season brought back memories of another more peaceful time.

THE TEMPERATURE ALARM clanged at midnight. Kate put on sweats, insulated coveralls and heavy boots. The kittens fussed at the activity and cuddled deeper into the down comforter. The dogs thumped their tails, but it was clear they had no intentions of going outside in the middle of the night. "You guys could at least keep me company," she said, yawning and picking up a flashlight.

A bright white moon rode high in the sky, creating a montage of silver pools and dark shadows. By the time she got to the strawberry field, the heavy dew was beginning to crystallize into glittering diamonds of ice. She turned the heavy ball valve at the irrigation station. The system spit and sputtered as the lines filled, then surged, and the sprinkler heads began to turn and spew out their lifesaving water. She sat on a bale of straw beside the field to watch and make sure all the sprinklers were operating properly.

By two o'clock, the icy field shimmered under the white moon, the only sound the *tick, tick, tick* of the sprinkler heads turning endlessly. As much as she hated frost nights, they never ceased to inspire awe. Particularly when the moon was bright and before her eyes the strawberry field turned into a magical fairy-land of diamonds and crystals.

She leaned back against the straw stack and dozed.

"I've read about it in books, but I've never seen it," Jay said, marveling. "It's beautiful."

Kate shook herself awake. "Yeah." Her voice was husky. "It is."

"Why didn't you call me?" he asked, sitting down beside her. "Do you have to stay out here all night?"

She shrugged. "Not really, but the temp's still dropping. Below twenty, the sprinklers could start freezing up. Or a pipe could break or—"

"You don't trust the system." He chewed on a piece of straw. "Will this hurt the blueberries?"

She shook her head. "They haven't broken bud yet. Blues can stand an amazing amount of cold."

"Another plus for the blues. This would wipe out grape buds." He fell silent. Then, "Kate, about the other night. I didn't mean—"

"I know," she said quickly, very much aware of his closeness. "I was tired. You were tired. People do weird things when they're tired."

"You think what passed between us was exhaustion?"

She squirmed against the straw.

He turned to face her. "Do you think we could start this conversation over again?"

"There's nothing to talk about." She stood. "I'd better check the temperature."

"I'll go with you."

"You don't need to."

"I am very much aware of what I need to do and what I don't need to do. Lord, can't you come off that 'I don't need anybody for anything' high horse for a few minutes?"

Kate started around the field. She didn't have to check the temperature or anything else. What she had to do was wake up and get away from the straw stack. Jay walked beside her, his balled fists shoved in his pockets.

"What kind of movies do you like?"

She gave him a quick sidelong glance. "I don't know. I don't go to movies much." She and Toby and gone to movies a lot. Since then...

"Well, if you went, what kind would you go to?"

She shrugged. "A good Western, with lots of horses and gunsmoke."

"They don't make good Westerns anymore," he said shaking his head. "Anything else?"

"Are you inviting me to a movie?" she asked suspiciously.

He stopped and faced her. "I guess not if we have to wait for a Western. Kate, I would like to see you someplace and sometime that doesn't have anything to do with farms and crops. That's all."

Kate started walking again, a bit faster now. "Why?" The calm of her voice belied the turmoil she felt inside. "I thought we settled all that."

"Why? Because... I like you." He kicked at the ground. "Because I want to get to know you. Because I can't get you out of my head no matter how hard I work at it."

"Look, there's nothing to get to know. This is it. Exciting nights in a strawberry field, days pruning blueberry bushes, dogs and cats..." Her voice trailed off, but when he didn't respond, she blundered on, unable to stand the silence. "I just don't think it's a good idea."

"What are you afraid of?"

"I'm not afraid of anything," she said angrily. "I just don't go out much." *Never* was closer to the truth, but she wasn't about to tell him that.

"Is that written in granite somewhere? A rule for life you invented along the way? Is it that you don't like men? Hate men?" He took her by the arm and turned her around to face him. "Or is it me?" he asked softly.

Kate took a deep breath and refused to look at him. "All of the above. What am I supposed to be doing while you're getting to know me so you can get me out of your head? I don't want to become involved with somebody who needs a diversion and who's going to take off next month or whenever." There. It was out.

He rubbed the back of his neck. "Ah. So you did overhear my telephone conversation that day," he said. "I wondered. I was talking to my sister, Beth, and you evidently heard only a part of the conversation. I have to go back to California in June for a couple of days, that's all. I'll do it before the harvest." He looked away from Kate, his body radiating tension. "You want a forty-year commitment before you'll even go out to a movie or dinner or a walk in the woods? A lifetime planned before you even explore the possibilities?"

"No. But it would be nice to know *something* about a man before..." Before what? Before you fall into bed with him? Or before you fall in love with him?

"I don't even know where to start."

"Why don't you start with what somebody like you is doing on a blueberry farm in—"

Something changed suddenly. Kate fell silent and held up a warning hand, cocking her head. She listened intently, her eyes scanning the field. At first glance, nothing was different. She could still hear the pump at the lake, and yet, within minutes, she was sure the sprinklers had slowed. Then one on the far end of the field sputtered and quit. "We're losing pressure," she said, and ran toward the irrigation station.

"What is it?" Jay called. "The regulator?"

"Yeah. We need crescent wrenches and a socket set." He nodded and sprinted past her.

The above-ground pressure gauge had dropped from a hundred pounds to fifty. Not enough to drive the sprinklers. The regulator was down in a manhole—one her father had constructed from a garbage can. She wrenched the lid off and shone her flashlight into the hole. She'd had trouble with this regulator before, but replacing it meant digging up a lot of line. She listened and knew that most of the sprinkler heads had stopped.

Jay dumped the tools beside the hole. "You think it's frozen up or shot?"

"We better hope frozen up. We've got thirty minutes."

"You hold the light," Jay said in a tense voice.

Kate shone the light to the far side of the buried can. "Watch out for Maheitabel."

"Who?" Then he saw it. "What the...? That's a black widow!." The glossy black spider moved, exposing its vivid red hourglass marking. Jay looked at

Kate. "You don't really expect me to put my hands down there."

"She won't hurt you. She's lived here for years." Kate pushed vainly at Jay. "I'll do it. She can't bite through gloves."

Jay took a deep breath and whipped out a pair of gloves. "I don't believe this," he said in an angry voice as he sprayed penetrating oil on the adjustment mechanism on top of the regulator. "What if you get bitten when you're out here in the middle of the night all by yourself?"

Kate handed him a wrench. "If she bit, which she won't, I'd have plenty of time to get help. You don't drop dead in two minutes. And don't yell. It disturbs her."

"Great," he whispered through clenched teeth.

"She eats flies and bugs, so she can't be all bad. What do you want me to do? Squash her?"

"The thought did occur to me." The tendons stood out on his neck as he applied pressure to the wrench. "Damn. This thing's rusted. You need a new one."

"I know that. Let the oil work a minute."

Jay squirted the bolt again and sat up. "I don't know another woman in the entire world who wouldn't be having hysterics if she found a black widow. I suppose you like snakes and mice, too?"

"I don't exactly like them, but we get along. If you want hysterical twits, a farm's the wrong place to look."

"I don't want hysterical twits," he said softly, and bent over the regulator again. "Hold on, Maheitabel. I'll be out of here in a minute." When he leaned on the wrench the bolt screamed, but it turned. "Which way?"

"All the way to the left, then come back to the right until I tell you to stop." She turned off the ball valve and watched the pressure gauge drop to zero. She heard the bolt on the regulator protest every turn Jay made and hoped it wouldn't break off.

"I'm starting back to the right."

Kate crossed her fingers and watched the gauge. When the needle began to creep upward she breathed again. "It's coming, it's coming. Stop." She heard Jay sit up, but kept her eyes glued to the gauge until it settled on the one-hundred mark and stayed. "Got it." She waited another minute to make sure it would hold, then turned the ball valve. The sprinkler heads spit and sputtered, then settled into their even *tick, tick, tick.*

Jay bent down again. "Sorry for the inconvenience, ma'am," he whispered, putting the lid back on the manhole.

Kate grinned in spite of herself. "I thank you and Maheitabel thanks you."

Jay chuckled and bent forward until his forehead rested on the ground. "Glad I could be of service to you ladies."

Kate laughed—and tumbled a little closer toward loving him. "Do you realize you have to be completely certifiably nuts to make a living this way?"

"Yes," he said quietly. "But when everything goes right and the vines are so heavy with fruit it hurts to look at them, it's the greatest high in the world."

The laughter was gone from his voice, replaced by something else—a longing, a wistfulness, she wasn't sure what. She only knew it was time to get away from him—before the moon and the magic of the ice muddled her brain. "Thanks for your help. I—"

"I know, you could have done it by yourself." He reached over and tapped her nose. "But wasn't it better with two?"

"I guess it was." She scrambled to her feet. "So. You were going to tell me something about your life in California."

"It's a long story, Kate. Too long for what's left of the night." He took her hand, and the image of both of them holding hands with grimy leather gloves on made her smile. "Tomorrow night—or I guess I mean tonight, assuming we're not out here baby-sitting the strawberries and your pet spider—we're going out. Somewhere special. I'll pick you up at six."

"Well, I—"

"I'm not trying to take over your farm, and I'm not going to run out in the middle of harvest." He took off a glove and tucked a strand of hair under her cap. "Am I getting close to what you're so afraid of?"

"No," she lied, alarmed at his perception. Toby had stood at almost this same spot one frosty night and told her that she was crazy to sit out here all night. That if she didn't trust the system, she should get another one. "You can't give your whole life to a bunch of plants," he'd said. She should have known then that Toby wasn't cut out for growing anything but cows, but she'd shrugged it off, sure that he would come to love this farm as much as she did. But Jay... Jay had offered to sit with her, which made her feel ... better. Not totally trusting yet, but better.

"Okay, but something's happening between us," Jay said gently. "I didn't want it, you don't want it, but it won't go away." He took her face in both hands. "I can't make you any promises, but dammit, I can't walk off. I have to see if . . . I have to see.'' He took a step back, then another. "Six o'clock."

She wanted to ask him what would happen if in time he didn't like what he saw, if in time he learned to hate blueberries, but she already knew the answer to that. He would go and she would stay—and try to piece a broken heart back together again. She watched him finally turn and walk off, head down, hands jammed in his pockets, as if he already regretted his words.

CHAPTER SEVEN

KATE SLEPT till midafternoon, but still woke up fuzzy-headed. Her internal clock always took two or three days to get over an all-nighter in the strawberry field. She stumbled down the stairs in search of coffee, knowing she ought to be worrying about Jay and dinner and what to wear, but she was too tired. The dogs lay sprawled on the couch, as if the long night had worn them out, too.

"I don't know what you guys are doing sleeping," she said. "All nice and cozy while I was out earning your keep." The kittens flew up the stairs, obviously untroubled by the intricacies of frosty nights and internal clocks.

She yawned and turned on the TV weather station, hoping for news of a warm front—preferably a fast-moving one. Two frost nights in a row were murder. Three nights, which had happened some years back, turned one into a zombie. But clouds were rolling in from the south, and Kate breathed easier. Clouds and a south wind would keep the temperature above freezing.

After coffee and a hot shower, she felt almost human again and up to rummaging in the closet. She settled on a calf-length wool skirt and a matching knit top. She even took extra time with her hair and dabbed on a bit of makeup. "He probably won't recognize me in a dress," she told the kittens. "*I* hardly recognize me in a dress."

When she opened the door at six, her greeting caught in her throat. Jay wore gray slacks and a double-breasted navy blazer she could tell was hand-tailored. A crisp white shirt heightened his California tan. He was gorgeous.

He leaned against the door. "You're staring. Is something unzipped or unbuttoned?"

"No. I'm not used to... You look very nice."

He let out a long low whistle as his eyes devoured her. "You look pretty nice yourself."

"Uh, where are we going?" she asked, gathering up her dress coat.

"There is not a Western to be found in town. However, according to the local paper, there's a charity dance at the Hilton in Fayetteville tonight. A real live big band. That means forties' music in case you didn't know, and it's one of my great loves." He lifted her hand and twirled her around. "We'll eat, then dance the night away."

"Dance?" Kate squeaked. As best she could remember, forties' music was cheek-to-cheek stuff, fancy steps, fox-trot, samba, and all very romantic. Which sounded great, but for one minor problem. She couldn't dance.

Dinner was elegant, except she didn't taste a bite of it, worrying about how they were going to kill three or four hours at a dance without dancing. In an effort to fortify herself, she consumed three glasses of wine, which was two over her usual limit. Jay was beside himself with delight at discovering a big band in the wilds of Arkansas. He spent a good part of dinner explaining the finer points of forties' music and throwing out names like Spivak and Barnett and Dorsey, none of whom she'd ever heard of. When she couldn't stand it a minute longer, she interrupted. "How come you know about forties' bands? I thought California was all heavy metal and acid rock."

"Mom and Dad. I was going to see Basie and Ellington when I was still a kid." He kissed the palm of her hand. "It's music for lovers."

"Oh, Lord," she muttered. Except for the all too familiar fire racing up her arm, she might as well be with a stranger trying to understand a foreign language.

"I'll bet your folks listened to the big bands."

"Try the Grand Ole Opry. Bill Monroe, Roy Acuff, Bob Wills and his Western swing band." She almost laughed at Jay's quizzical look. "Different planets."

The ballroom at the Hilton was decorated with balloons, streamers and cozy tables with candles. All Kate saw was the enormous dance floor.

The banner stretched over the bandstand read DANCE TO THE MUSIC OF JACK TERRY AND THE BIG BAND. Kate and Jay, of course, were early enough to get a table right next to the dance floor. "They look like the Medicare crowd," she said, referring to the age of most of the musicians. Maybe she could convince Jay the band was awful before they started playing.

But Jay's eyes twinkled like a kid's at Christmas. "I'll bet every one of them played with one of the *real* big bands." When she grunted, he shook his head. "These guys are all that's keeping this music alive, Kate. There are a few younger groups, but it's tough to make a living."

The bandleader introduced the band and thanked everyone for coming to support the local free clinic, then opened with a loud brassy number. "'One O'clock Jump'!" Jay exclaimed. "The Count."

"Are we talking Dracula or what?"

"Count Basie. My man," he said, swaying to the beat. "This band could swing anywhere."

Kate watched a dozen couples in their sixties take to the floor, executing the complicated whirls and swirls, dips and gyrations that Jay explained was classic jitterbug.

He pointed to a white-haired couple who went through a series of complex steps so smoothly it was obvious they'd been doing it forever. "The Lindy hop. It's a jitterbug, but has unique steps." He took her hand. "Dance?"

"Too fast," she said quickly. She begged off the second one—"Too Spanish." The third—"Never did like that song." The band slowed the tempo with "I'll Never Smile Again."

Jay turned to her. "Does this one suit you?"

"Um, I don't know."

"The reason people go to dances is to dance." He studied her face. "You don't know how, do you?"

She looked at the tablecloth and shook her head.

He pulled her to her feet. "It's time you learned."

"Not in front of all these people," she hissed.

"These people aren't interested in us. Come on."

She increased her resistance. "I probably need about four bottles of wine before I'm ready."

"They *will* be interested, however, if I drag you out on the floor."

"You wouldn't."

"I would." He led her onto the floor. "Just relax and go where I go."

Kate tried to relax, tried to follow him, but her feet kept getting tangled up with his. She felt like a gangly newborn calf.

"Relax, you'll get the hang of it. I can't believe you've missed out on one of the true delights in life."

She tried to concentrate on what his feet were doing. "This isn't exactly the culture capital of the world."

He pulled her closer. "Mad will not help you relax. It's like making love—slow, easy and sweet."

The thought of making love to him made her stumble. "I'm not mad."

"You must have gone to dances in college."

"Mostly country and western or rock. You just wiggle around in the general vicinity of your partner. I almost learned the two-step once." But she *was* beginning to enjoy the sensation of being in his arms, his body pressed against hers.

He swept her around. "You'll be addicted before the night's over," he promised.

By the time they played "Polka Dots and Moonbeams" she had quit thinking about his feet and her feet, and admitted she loved the music. After intermission, during which Jay talked to the band leader and she had a few more sips of wine, he led her through a relatively slow jitterbug.

"Jack Terry's from San Francisco. He played with the Russ Morgan Band," Jay said when they sat down. "Oh, I would love to show you San Francisco. Food you wouldn't believe. Little clubs with some of the finest jazz in the world." His eyes glittered with excitement.

"You must miss it," she murmured, thinking about how different their worlds were once they got off the farm.

"I hate cities for living in. But San Francisco is one of the great cities of the world for visiting."

"You spend a lot of time there?"

He shrugged. "In my younger days. Not so much in recent years. It's better when someone enjoys it with you."

She couldn't help but notice the tinge of bitterness in his voice, and he effectively ended the conversation by asking if she wanted more wine.

"Club soda, maybe." She knew without his telling her that there had been someone special who wasn't special anymore. Was that who he was running away from? He was threading his way back from the bar when someone hugged her from behind.

"It *is* you lurking over here. And in a dress, yet."

She twisted around to see Barry, then noticed that Jay had stopped to watch them. "Let me go, Barry, or I'll scream."

"So testy these days," he said, dropping his hands and sitting down at the table. "That, I presume, is the neighborhood hunk?" he asked, motioning toward Jay.

Kate gave serious consideration to sliding under the table and staying there for the duration. "I didn't invite you to sit down." She examined his flushed face in the dim light. "Did you get an early start on the festivities?"

"I've been here for hours. And you can't run me off. I'm one of the sponsors for this bash." He stood up as Jay approached the table. "You must be Jay. I'm Barry Wade."

As they shook hands, Jay was smiling and Barry was smiling, and Kate had the distinct impression they were sizing each other up.

"So how do you like Arkansas?" Barry asked in what was supposed to be his hard-edged courtroom voice. The words came out a bit slurred.

"Fine."

"How long are you staying?"

Kate kicked Barry under the table. "Save your Perry Mason routine for the courtroom. Barry's a lawyer," she said for Jay's benefit. "And a neighbor. We grew up together."

"I proposed to Kate when she was seven."

"Barry!"

Barry leered at Kate. "Well, I'm sure he's heard all about it from Gladys. He practically lives there."

"I refused, of course," she said sweetly to Jay. "For obvious reasons. Will you excuse us a minute?" She yanked Barry out of his chair and dragged him toward the door. "Barry Wade, you haven't been this obnoxious since you got drunk at the junior prom. Why isn't Angie here to keep you company?"

"She's working. It's my duty to look after you, Kate."

"Look after me? You can't even look after yourself. Now get lost." She started back toward the table.

He followed. "I demand to know his intentions toward you."

"I don't believe this. Do I go around spying on Angie and Kitty and crew?"

"Well, no, but—"

"But nothing. We all have to screw up our lives as we see fit. Now go home and go to bed."

Barry sighed. "I can't. I have to stay till this stupid thing's over."

"Then go find some coffee."

"Kate, sweet, I'm only trying to help."

"I know." She reached up and bussed his cheek.

When she got back to the table, Jay was deep in thought. His face looked as if it was carved in stone, the frown etched there permanently. "He's had a bit too much wine," she said brightly.

"How long has he been in love with you?"

"Since forever," she said, trying to read what was in his eyes. "But he's not really. He just thinks he is."

"You're wrong."

"No, I'm not."

"You were engaged." It wasn't a question.

"At age seven and nine. I don't think that counts. Look, Gladys is probably trying to create a little competition. She thinks if you—"

"It makes a lot of sense, the two of you."

"It doesn't make any sense to me, and that's the end of the discussion." She sipped her soda, watching him. He was strangely quiet and she wondered what was going on in his mind. She knew he was fighting some inner turmoil that threatened to finish the evening.

He smiled at last, but it was a different smile; tight and controlled. "I guess I haven't earned the right to be jealous, have I?"

She leaned over and straightened his collar. "I don't think there's anything to be jealous of," she said quietly, sensing he was trying to force himself to relax.

"The evening's young and you're so beautiful." He smiled. "Sounds like a good song title, doesn't it?"

The band began to play again. "I recognize this one!" she crowed. "It's 'Stardust.'"

He grinned, pulling her onto the dance floor and into his arms. "Artie Shaw's great recording?"

She laughed into his chest. "Willie Nelson."

"I might have known."

She let his scent and warmth envelop her. Since it was the last set, the band continued playing at a slow tempo. Kate stayed in Jay's arms, pressed against him, until the crowd dwindled and only a few dancers remained on the floor. But for Kate there was only the music and Jay. She was so happy she worried that this was a Cinderella story, and that at midnight it would all disappear. As if he could read her mind, Jay pulled her closer. The thought that they might never experience a moment like this again terrified her.

"I guess you miss all your friends in California, don't you?" she murmured against his chest, desperate to quell her growing fears. "And you must have family."

His sure gliding steps faltered and he held her so tight she could hardly breathe. "I have a son out there, Kate."

Kate's head spun like a carousel out of control. "A son?" she asked, struggling to keep from tearing herself away from the warmth and safety of his arms.

He pulled her still tighter as they swayed to the music. "Does that bother you?"

"Of course not," she said, but her mind reeled to adjust to the news. "It's just a surprise, I guess. You must miss him very much."

"I do." His eyes sought hers. "He's six."

In the next few minutes, he told her about his son—that she would like him, that his name was Luke and he loved farms. Jay told her other things, but Kate was too devastated by the implications of his revelation to hear them all. Jay had a son! Which meant that of course he would go back home to California! A man like Jay could never stand long-term separation from his child. And she suddenly understood the source of his anger and pain. He hadn't mentioned his ex-wife, or even if she was an ex. Oh, Lord, how would she bear it when he left?

A SLEEPLESS NIGHT did little to improve her outlook. When Barry called at seven, she'd been up for hours.

"Sorry if I was a jerk at the dance, Kate."

"You were, but all is forgiven," she said, trying to sound normal.

"When you have to hang around and smile for hours, it gets boring. But I'm glad to see you out and about even if it's not with me. And by the by, that Jay person is *not* some itinerant farmhand. He's well educated, comes from money, and he's madly in love with you."

Kate fought back tears. "Barry, I don't—"

"But the burning question is, are you in love with him? And more to the point, what are you and he going to do about it?"

"Absolutely nothing. Good grief, Barry, you sound like a Victorian father."

"If you won't tell me, I'll ask him."

"You do, and I will never speak to you again."

Barry's voice became serious. "Forget everything I just said. I'm here if you want to talk, Kate, day or night. Lord knows I've bent your ear enough."

It was tempting, but... "Thanks. Maybe later."

She drank coffee and paced the house, trying to make sense of her tumultuous thoughts, but it always came back to one thing. Even if Jay was beginning to... love her a little bit—something she wasn't at all sure about—he had a son two thousand miles away. Too far away for a weekend visit, a special day at school, a ball game. She'd be a fool to think he could ever give up all that to stay with her. She couldn't imagine how he'd managed it for this long. And could she give up the farm, the life she loved, if he asked? It was a question for which she had no answer.

CHAPTER EIGHT

THREE NIGHTS LATER, Kate sat on her front porch, watching a full moon rise over the river. It seemed impossibly large, a rich golden orb you could almost reach out and touch. The night was warm and busy with the sounds of insects awakened from their long sleep. It was the first time in three days that she'd relaxed, the first time she'd given herself over to thoughts about Jay. She had, after the dance, thrown herself into the hardest dirtiest work she could find, work that numbed the mind, along with the body.

She'd seen Jay once, and that had been to ask him about the irrigation pump. But he'd been distant and preoccupied. Maybe he thought she couldn't accept a child, but it was the child's residence, not the child, that bothered her. And the question of where Jay belonged. And whether he'd even hang around long enough for the harvest. Of couse, maybe it had come home to him, too, what different worlds they lived in, how little they knew about each other. Or maybe thoughts of Barry nagged at him. Or...

Whatever the reasons, he was struggling with *some* demon. And there was so little time left to work things out. The strawberries would be ready to pick in a week. After the strawberries were harvested they'd be into the blueberries, and then there wouldn't be a spare minute for anything.

She'd been starting to think that Jay was beginning to work through some of his anger and pain, beginning to relax and enjoy life a bit. Maybe even starting to settle into a new life. Although a nagging voice kept muttering that was wishful thinking, she'd been unable to conjure up an image of him living anywhere else. But one evening in a ballroom and images popped up like rabbits out of a hat. Clubs, concerts, elegant restaurants. The image of Jay as a father. How long could he find contentment away from the life he'd grown up with? How long could he stay here, so far from his child?

Tonight she'd discovered several things about herself. The first was that, sometime when she wasn't looking, she'd fallen head over heels in love. The second was that the day might come when she would have to decide whether or not she could leave this farm and the life she'd so carefully built.

Jay was everything she'd ever dreamed of in a man. But she was a farm girl, and so firmly rooted in the flintrock hills of Arkansas she couldn't imagine living anywhere else, couldn't imagine the world he so comfortably drifted in and out of. Buried deep inside was the fear that she wouldn't measure up in a place like California.

She chided herself. He hadn't given her any reason to think she'd ever have to, so why was she worrying herself sick? It was going to hurt like hell when he left whether he loved her and asked her to go, or was indifferent and didn't ask her to go, or—

She sat upright at the sound of a howl. The dogs tumbled off the porch and ran down the drive barking wildly. The cacophony made her clap her hands over her ears. Bemused, she watched as Jay, flanked by an excited Chester and Molly, ambled toward her.

"Why aren't you howling?" Jay asked, totally deadpan, when he reached the foot of the steps.

Her blood ran hot at the sight of him. Was this his way of asking if things were all right? She raised her head and howled, exciting the dogs, who ran between them, barking madly, even further.

Kate laughed. "What's the occasion?"

Jay made a sweeping bow. "Full moon. I came to carry you off into the forest." He arched one eyebrow and twiddled one end of a villainous imaginary mustache. "At which time, my dear, I shall have my way with you."

"Sir, I am not in the habit of being carried off to the woods." She clutched a hand to her breast. "But I'll tell you, it's the best offer I've had all day."

With a flourish he produced a bottle of wine and a bouquet of rather wilted dandelions. "A little worse for wear, I fear, but the pickings are slim between my house and yours." When he offered her the flowers, the dogs sat down, disappointed that the game was over.

"That's because I am conscientious in my weed-control program. I hope the wine's in better shape."

"Come on, Katherine Ann Harmon," Jay whispered. "We're going for a walk."

Kate held the dandelions to her breast. "It's dark," she said, hesitating. In fact she'd spent many a spring evening wandering around the farm, but had never told anyone for fear of being laughed at.

"How can you say that under a moon like this?" He reached up and took her hand. "In my wanderings, I discovered a bluff over the river that I believe may be magical when the moon is full." He kissed her palm. "Do you believe in magic, Katherine?"

"Maybe," she said softly. She followed him, intoxicated by the pull of the moon and the even stronger pull of this man. Fingers entwined, they strolled past the strawberry field and on past the lake, which lay still and serene, like a magic mirror of silver that had captured the moon for its own. On through a wild meadow once ruled by an orchard, ruled now by quail and rabbits and Queen Anne's Lace. Finally to the limestone bluff that stood eighty feet above the river.

The bluff had once been her favorite playground. She and her friends had held off countless bands of Indians, gangsters and just plain old "bad guys" from their king-of-the-castle fortress. The top of the bluff was worn smooth from centuries of rain and sun, but the rugged face was still a favorite summer haunt of rock climbers. Every time Kate looked down the cracked limestone face, she marveled anew that she and her numerous playmates hadn't broken their necks playing on this part of the river.

Jay sat down cross-legged near the edge of the bluff and produced a plastic cup from his jacket pocket. He poured some wine and handed her the cup. "I didn't have room for another one. We'll have to share."

She sipped the wine, then passed him the cup. The moon had lost its deep golden glow, fading to pale yellow on its way to a ghostly white. The river was a ribbon of silver winding through dark woods and open pastures, where shadowy cows lay content, their bellies full of lush spring grass. Although Kate had stood on this bluff hundreds of times, it was different tonight. A shadow drifted over the moon and Kate pointed to a great horned owl floating silently past the bluff, down toward the pastures in search of food.

"He's enormous," Jay said, his voice filled with awe.

"He's been around for years, but you rarely get a glimpse of him."

"An owl is a good omen." He gently pulled her down in front of him. "Don't you feel the magic?"

She sat cross-legged, facing him, and when their knees touched, she felt more than magic. She hadn't done anything this silly and wonderful for years. "Maybe a little."

He leaned forward and put his hands around hers on the cup, tipped it to his lips, then to hers. The intimacy of the simple act loosened a flood of emotion in Kate.

"Only a little?" Entwining his fingers in her hair, he pulled her close and kissed her. "I've missed you."

"I've missed you, too." She felt the warmth of the wine mingle with the heat of his lips and wanted this moment to last forever.

"What are you so afraid of?" he asked softly. When she didn't answer, he sighed and drew away. After a long moment, he offered her the cup again.

She took a sip, but what she wanted was the warmth of his kisses, not the wine. She shivered and tried to say something—anything—but couldn't.

He touched her lips with his finger. "Is the problem a little boy you don't even know?"

She shook her head, not quite ready to talk about her fears or bare her soul. Attempting a smile, she asked, "What happened to the villain?"

He poured more wine and took a long swallow. "He's sitting in front of you." He paused. "You know nothing about the man inside. . . ."

She put a finger to his lips. "Maybe I know too much."

He shook his head. "When I kiss you, I feel something I haven't felt in a long time, and it scares me. And I see the same fear in your eyes. Who was he?"

Kate bit her lip and decided maybe it *was* time to do some soul-baring. Only her parents knew what had happened with Toby, and even they didn't know that he'd begged her to come to Oklahoma and that she'd refused. "We were at the university together. I was a freshman and he was a senior the fall he started working for us. Mom and Dad had built their new house, and I'd bought the old farmhouse to go with my twenty acres—my dream farm." She hesitated at first, but as the moon rose high on its solitary trek west, the words and feelings poured out.

"He didn't want to go back to his dad's cattle operation. He wanted glamour farming, and at that time blueberries were considered a glamour crop. High returns, guaranteed market." She smiled and traced patterns on the smooth rock with her finger. "He didn't make it through the harvest. Didn't even make it to peak week. After twenty-hour days and several crises, he decided cows looked pretty good. Thinking back, I suspect he was planning on getting his hands on the big farm one day and turning it into a cattle operation."

She shook off the painful memories. "I hear he's running his dad's ranch now. He wanted me to come with him." She looked up and her gaze locked with Jay's. "I couldn't do it."

"You loved him, but you didn't respect him anymore, right?" He stroked her cheek. "I'm not asking you to give up this place, Kate. I'm asking you to walk down this road a ways with me, see where it leads us." He smiled. "And I *have* been through a few harvests. Like a grape harvest every year since I can remember."

But she was still gun-shy about harvest. Picking clusters of wine grapes was one thing, but picking a zillion little blueberries—one berry at a time—and getting them packed and shipped was another. The blues were very labor intensive. "But don't you see how different our worlds are?" she cried. "You like Count Basie, I like Willie Nelson. You're...sophisticated and worldly, I'm a farm girl." She reached out to smooth the crease from his brow. "It scares me. You're tied to California, I'm tied to Arkansas."

"The only time I don't think I belong in Arkansas is when you tell me. Or when I see you with Barry and know you'd grow old and comfortable together with tons of kids and grandkids." He leaned forward and brushed her lips with his. "I don't have a crystal ball that foretells the next twenty years. Can't we live in the present for now and let the future take care of itself?"

And what about the little boy she didn't know? How could he not worry about that? "What are you so scared of?" she said, hoping that for once Jay would open up.

"Women. Getting close to someone." He sipped wine and handed her the cup. "Nasty divorce. Nastier custody and property battle. I lost my vineyard, and when I didn't get joint custody of Luke, I went a little crazy." He sighed. "It's a long story."

She could feel the tension emanating from him and knew that whatever had happened, it was still too painful to talk about. "I'm sorry."

"I have Luke this summer. Is that a problem?"

"Of course not."

"I want to keep him till September, but from what my sister tells me, it may be a rocky three months. Jennifer, my ex-wife, has been teaching him to hate me from what I hear." He pulled Kate to him, and this time his kiss was long and lingering and hungry. "I didn't want to like you, Kate Harmon. I didn't ever want to feel this way about a woman again. But you..." He shook his head. "There are so many words that need saying."

"Jay," she said, silencing him with a kiss. "You're right. We do need to talk. But first we both need to do some serious thinking. And there's no chance for that with harvest looming ahead. Why don't we see if we can make it through harvest together. If we can get through that, we'll have all the time we need for talking." And maybe by then she wouldn't melt every time he touched her.

He stood up and pulled her to her feet. "Okay. No more serious subjects tonight. Just us and the moon." He cupped her chin and looked deep into her eyes. "But don't forget, I know all about the stresses of a harvest. They may be different for blues, but I can handle them just fine."

Kate shivered. She'd heard that line before.

KATE AND GEORGE were scrubbing counters and washing buckets at the sales stand when her parents' motor home lumbered up the driveway. "I wasn't expecting you till late," she said, hugging her mother and scolding the dogs for barking and jumping on everyone.

Sarah Harmon pointed to her husband. "We haven't slowed down since Mississippi. Afraid he'd miss the whole season if we stopped for lunch."

Leonard Harmon looked sheepish. "Didn't see any need to stop." He kissed Kate, then gestured at the vehicle. "Besides, once this thing got her nose pointed toward home, she didn't want to stop."

"Quit blaming that poor old machine," Sarah chided. "It was you got a whiff of home and couldn't bear to stop."

"Your mother's a joy to travel with, honey," Leonard said, winking at Kate.

Kate realized how much she'd missed them. "I'm glad to see you two carrying on like always. There's food at the house, but go easy. Gladys has killed the fatted calf and Lord only knows what else for supper tonight."

George approached. "Right fair crop this year, Leonard. Guess you lost the knack for work, bein' down *there* all winter."

"I'll work you into the ground this summer, George."

"Wouldn't take much," George retorted. "Missy, here, like to worked me to death this winter."

Kate urged her parents to go eat and rest, but Leonard just smiled. "Soon's I look in on my machinery."

Kate intercepted him. She hadn't told her parents that Luther Thomas had never made it to Arkansas or that she'd hired a farm manager. She'd hoped to spring these tidbits at supper when her father was rested. However, since Jay was working in the shed, she had to explain his presence. "Dad, Luther's been delayed and sent me money to hire someone. The guy working in there is the one. His name's Jay," she said rapidly, figuring if she talked fast enough her father wouldn't notice a few major gaps.

"Whoa, girl." Leonard turned, frowning. "What delayed him?"

Kate smiled. "I don't know exactly. Just a business delay, I guess."

But Leonard wasn't satisfied. "This Jay know anything about machinery?"

"He's very good with machinery and everything else he touches. I'll tell you all about it later."

"The boy's a right good worker, even if he is from California," George said.

Leonard muttered that he'd see about that and walked toward the shed. Kate tucked her mother's arm in hers and started toward the house. "How's Dad doing?"

"If he was doing any better, I couldn't stand him." Sarah sighed. "He's been chomping at the bit to get home since January. I don't think he'll ever go back to Florida. He says the place is nothing but a bunch of old Republicans waiting to die, and he plans to die among Democrats and blueberries, not Republicans and Winnebagos."

Kate stopped. "Great. So what do we do now?"

"I don't know, honey. But I'm sure glad we're out from under the farm." She gave Molly a playful shove. "He's talking about buying a place. A *little* place. Now what's this about Luther being delayed?"

Kate leaned closer to her mother. "I wish I knew. I haven't heard a word from him, except for a couple of little notes and big checks."

"What do you think it is?"

Kate shrugged. "I can't imagine. The notes just said he'd been delayed. I've left messages, but he's never called back." When she said it out loud, it sounded worse than ever. Over the weeks, she'd mostly quit thinking about Luther's absence. Jay was handling the farm as if he'd grown up on it, so she'd simply laid the whole problem of Luther Thomas aside. But her father wasn't going to shrug it off so easily, even if the farm was no longer his concern. A born worrywart, he would drive her crazy until he got some answers. Answers she didn't have.

Sarah frowned. "Strange, isn't it?"

"Yeah, it is. By the way, there are a couple of furry persons at the house you haven't met yet. They're at the destructive stage."

Sarah dismissed this bit of news with a shrug. "So what else is new? Now where on earth did you find a farm manager who could take care of the place?"

Kate smiled and hugged her mother. "*That* is a long story, Mom."

THAT NIGHT, Gladys and Sarah ran everyone out of the kitchen, saying too many cooks spoiled the broth—or in this case, the gravy. But Kate knew it was so they could catch up on their visiting. She wandered into the living room, but her father and Jay were deep in a discussion on the relative merits of various kinds of ultralight planes. Their conversation was easy, as if they'd known each other for years.

"I took lessons in a two-seater Challenger," Leonard said. "I'd love to have my own."

"I'd rather have a Tierra. Or a Phantom."

"I heard about them. I'm going to sneak over to Oklahoma one of these Saturdays. I hear they got a lot of clubs over there. But not a word to Sarah."

"I'll sneak over with you," Jay whispered in a conspiratorial voice.

Kate smiled, wondering how her father planned to hide an airplane. He'd come back from the shed that afternoon and said she'd "done good," although he couldn't imagine how a fellow like Jay had ever found a blueberry farm in Arkansas. Sometimes, in the quiet dark of the night, Kate wondered the same thing.

Gladys's voice floated out of the kitchen. "Leonard Harmon, you and I are going to have a very serious talk about old fools who think they can fly."

"Damn woman's got ears like radar," Leonard muttered.

"She'll tie you to a tree if you're not careful, Daddy," Kate said just as Sarah called them to eat.

Leonard rubbed his hands when he saw the table. "Lord, I haven't sat down to a meal like this since I left."

Sarah patted her husband's stomach—which was less ample than a year ago, but still very much in evidence. "Poor dear. Just wasting away for lack of a good meal."

Leonard sucked in his stomach. "Well, that stuff you been feeding me wouldn't keep a bird alive."

"Might not keep a bird alive, but it'll keep a heart patient alive." Sarah turned to Gladys. "Strict low-fat, low-cholesterol. He hates it."

Gladys began to fuss. "Well, you should have told me."

"If he sat down to your table and found a bunch of steamed vegetables, he'd go berserk and kill us all," Sarah said with a twinkle in her eye.

Leonard spooned gravy onto almost everything. "If God had meant us to live without gravy, he wouldn't have put women like Gladys on this earth."

Gladys beamed. "If you're going to fall out of the sky, Leonard, you need a full stomach."

Kate had missed these dinners, first at Gladys's, then at Sarah's, sometimes at Mary Beth's. She glanced at Jay, who was eating like a horse and taking in every word, a smile playing on his lips.

"Well," Gladys announced, patting his arm, "you can't believe what a godsend this dear boy has been. I don't know what Kate would have done without him."

Jay bent to his food and Kate wished she was close enough to kick Gladys under the table.

"Oh, don't blush, Jay. You know it's the truth. I almost worried myself to death with Kate all by herself on that farm. Why, she could have been killed in her sleep."

"I am perfectly capable of taking care of myself," Kate said through clenched teeth. She had an awful feeling that Gladys was getting ready to launch into a lengthy monologue on Jay, on her, on romance, and probably end with plans for the wedding. "Is anyone ready for dessert?" she asked with false brightness.

Gladys didn't even break stride. "Don't be silly, dear. We haven't made a dent on the roast yet. I've slept like a top since Jay came to live with her."

"Gladys!"

"Oh, you know what I mean." She rolled her eyes at Sarah. "Goodness, children are *so* touchy these days. Anyway, I've told Jay that I won't hear of him traipsing back to California."

Kate knew that wedding plans were next on Gladys's agenda, so she jumped up and informed them all that *she* was ready for dessert, and furthermore, if they did less talking and more eating, *they* would be ready, too. "Jay and I are off to fix it," she announced, and hurried to the kitchen. Jay was hot on her heels, struggling to keep from laughing.

"It's not funny," she said, glaring at him. "I'm trying to decide if it's good manners to kill your hostess before dessert."

"Hmm, I think Emily Post would definitely say after dessert," he said. "Miss Manners might go for before." He stopped her retort with a light kiss. "I think it's a great idea."

"What? Killing Gladys?"

"Not traipsing back to California." His finger traced intricate patterns down her arm while she got out plates for the pie. "Have you thought about that possibility?"

"More to the point, have *you* thought about it? Really thought things through?" She ducked away from his tantalizing finger. "Don't do that. How am I supposed to keep my mind on pie when you keep touching me?"

He turned her around. This time the kiss was longer. "I don't need to think about anything. Except you," he whispered. "Why is it so different for you?"

"Because I come from a long line of worrywarts," she whispered, wishing she could stand right here wrapped in his arms forever. "I think we better slice the pie."

His voice changed, the tone hardened. "If you don't want me to stay, say so."

"Of course I want you to stay, but it's not that simple. There are other people to think about." She sighed. "I don't know if I could go anywhere else. Except to get the ice cream. While you slice the pie."

"Did I say you should go anywhere? I thought we were talking about me staying here." When she didn't respond, he closed his eyes and shook his head. His voice softened. "I want to be where you are, Kate."

Her breath caught in her throat, and any argument she had died on her lips. Was he saying he loved her? Not exactly, but... "I thought we were going to talk about this later. Like after harvest."

"We are." He coaxed a smile with his finger. "Just tell me one thing. What do you want?"

She groaned, wondering how she was going to get through the rest of the evening with his words rocketing around in her brain. "You. And the pie. Before Gladys comes to see why we're taking so long."

"Gladys would approve."

"But Mom and Dad. And—"

"Get the ice cream," he said in a grim voice. "But let me tell you, this conversation is far from over."

"Okay. Little slices. Daddy's cholesterol."

He bussed her cheek. "You're worried about cholesterol after *that* meal?"

"You have to start somewhere." She tore herself away, knowing if she didn't they would never get the pie and ice cream served. Her heart was galloping along like a runaway team. If she had one ounce of romantic fantasy in her blood, she'd tell him she loved him and follow him to the ends of the earth or California or wherever. *If you weren't such a scaredy cat,* a small voice taunted. She bent down and stuck her head in the freezer.

After dinner Leonard and Jay went out, ostensibly to check some machine. "Gone off to moon over those airplane magazines Leonard keeps hidden in the motor home," Sarah said as the women worked in the kitchen.

When the kitchen sparkled again, Kate announced that she was going to bed. Sarah hugged Gladys and thanked her for a lovely welcome home.

"I'm not doing any more welcome backs, Sarah," Gladys chided. "You and Leonard need to stay where you belong."

As they left Gladys's, Kate was dying to ask her mother what she thought of Jay. She'd almost screwed up her courage when Sarah brought it up. "Jay seems like a remarkable young man. Is Gladys just doing some wishful thinking again, or is there something going on between you two?"

"Maybe," Kate said softly. "I like him a lot."

Sarah laughed. "Some of the looks you exchanged seemed to me as if it's gone way past 'like.'"

"Mom! You're not supposed to notice things like that."

"Honey, you'd be surprised at what I notice. Leonard's quite taken with your young man, and that's a real feat. How in the world did he get to Arkansas?"

"Blew in on a February breeze." They walked in silence for a time. "Oh, Mom, it's so complicated." She spilled out the story of his divorce, his son. "He says he wants to stay here. I don't know what to tell him."

"If it's that awful Toby you're thinking about, just quit it. Jay is a different kettle of fish. Listen to your heart, honey. And listen to him."

Kate wanted to tell her mother all the things she felt, what she dreamed about, what she was afraid of. "Mom, I just can't think straight right now. I want him to stay, but I don't want to feel guilty. Most of all, I don't want to do something I'll regret—or he'll regret."

Sarah put her hand on Kate's shoulder and gently shook her. "If you love each other, these things get worked out. That is, if you don't worry them into the ground. Now we'd best go drag your father off to bed. He'd rather die than admit he's worn-out."

They found the men in the shed, poring over ultralight magazines. "And I thought you two were working on something important," Sarah said, hands on her hips.

"We are, woman. Now leave us be," Leonard grumped as he tried to hide the magazines.

"Leave you be, my foot. You're going to bed, old man."

"I got too many years on me to need a nursemaid." He winked at Kate. "Jay and me figured there's just about enough room between the two farms for a landing strip. What do you think about that? 'Course, Luther would have to approve, but if he didn't, we could take out a couple of rows of blues."

"Not *my* blues," Kate said.

Sarah rolled her eyes. "I think you got gravy on the brain. Now get a move on."

"This boy's a real pilot. He can give me lessons." Leonard rubbed his jaw. "'Course, we'd have to have a plane."

Kate was trying to keep from laughing at the expression on Jay's face. He probably assumed her folks were about to come to blows. This was Sarah and Leonard's way, but it was a shock to outsiders. They snipped and threw jabs, but beneath the banter was a deep abiding love that many people only dreamed of. She went up and kissed her father. "You better go before she gets out the horsewhip," she whispered loudly.

"She's still not big enough to whip me, Katie. In spite of what she might think."

"I wouldn't take any odds on that."

Leonard closed his magazine. "See what happens when you're outnumbered by women? They gang up on a man."

Jay leaned close to the older man, smiling for the first time since the exchange started. "I don't think even the two of us can take them on. They probably don't fight fair." He slapped Leonard on the back. "We'll finish in the morning."

Kate walked to the shed door with her parents. "The downstairs bedroom's all made up, but close the door. The kittens love feet."

Sarah nodded and bustled her husband out into the night before he could ask why Kate wasn't coming. Jay turned off the overhead lights.

"Is that what happens after you're married a long time?" Jay asked.

She shrugged. "I think they were that way from the day they got together. Both strong and independent."

He put his arm around her. "Take a walk?"

"I didn't know you were a pilot," she said, hoping to head him off any further talk of the future. She wanted to savor what might be, not talk about it.

"An extravagance of my younger days. Am I to assume we're not going to pursue our earlier conversation?"

She put her arm around his waist and leaned against him, marveling as always at how well they fit. "Short walk. We open for strawberries in three days and I'm not ready. As usual."

"You'll get there. Ignoring us isn't going to change the way I feel, you know." He tucked her head under his chin. "I think, lovely lady, that you might love me. Just a little. I also think you're scared to admit it."

"How can you do this to me this close to the season?" she wailed.

"Out of my control." Near the river the great horned owl called. "He sounds sad tonight," Jay murmured. "You think it's because he's alone?"

"Maybe. I haven't heard a second one this spring." She snuggled a little closer to his warmth. They stopped by the strawberry field, where huge luscious berries were well on their way to deep crimson ripeness.

"Want to talk about strawberries? That's safe." He bent and cupped a cluster in his hand. "I've never seen a prettier field."

Kate swelled with pride. "Coming from somebody from California, that's a real compliment."

"Speaking of California, I have to pick up Luke in early June. I'll only be gone for a weekend, and we should be through strawberries by then, right?"

She nodded before she realized what he'd said. "We? Wait a minute. You have plenty to do on the big farm, and I can't pay you as much as Mr. Thomas, and—"

He pulled her head against the hollow of his shoulder and buried his face in her hair. "I'm ready for the blues. And you don't have to pay me anything."

She pulled away and looked up at him. "Oh, no. I pay the people who work for me." They'd never talked about money, but if he'd lost everything in the divorce—

He gathered her close again. "Don't you ever just let people help you out?"

"Sometimes. I mean, you could work in my flower garden for no pay, but—"

"But business is business. Okay, so I'll work for whatever your going rate is." He resumed walking. "No more arguments. I admire your obsession with honesty, but don't you think I've earned the right to help out when I want to?"

Kate thought their relationship was all the more reason she should keep everything aboveboard. Why, she wasn't exactly sure; it just seemed like the thing to do. "In answer to your original question, yes, we'll be into the blues by then and we should have plenty of help."

He nudged her chin up. "You know you've turned my world upside down, don't you?"

Her heart skipped a beat, then kicked into overdrive. "Yeah. You've kind of done the same thing to mine." His kiss was sudden and fierce and possessive, a demand for an answer. She buried her hands in his hair, kissing him back.

Jay pulled away at last, fighting for control. "Do you know how much I want you?" He shuddered and his breath came ragged and harsh in the quiet spring night. "We better walk some more."

Kate wasn't sure she could take another step. Her legs seemed to have turned from bone and muscle to something strongly resembling jelly. She struggled to control her own need. "What's your son like?"

"I'm not sure I know how to answer that. I haven't seen him since January."

"That's awful."

"Yeah. I lost my vineyard, which I can live without, but dammit, I want my son. At least one weekend a month plus the summers." He laughed bitterly. "I'm on trial this summer. If it doesn't go well, I don't know what'll happen."

They turned back toward the house, and her mother's question echoed through her head. "How *did* you end up here?"

"I knew if I stayed out there I'd show up at Luke's school one afternoon just to see him or go to one of his soccer games and do something stupid. So I got in the truck and headed east. I..." He hesitated, looking at her for a long moment, then shook his head. "I'd read about Arkansas blueberries in a trade journal. Figured I could bury myself on a farm for a few months."

Her heart ached for his loss. His farm, his son—no wonder he'd been been in such pain. But harvest was almost upon them, full of stress and frantic activity. It wasn't the time to add more strain. To his life—or to hers.

"Well," she said at last, "we're about to get buried in tons of big red berries, followed by zillions of little blueberries. When we come up for air..."

He cupped her face, kissing her eyes, her cheeks, her chin. "Sweet, practical, cautious Kate. The season is a long time."

She smiled. "But if we can get through the harvest together, we can get through anything."

"Okay. After the season. We'll sit down and I'll lay my sordid past at your feet and you can decide. There are things that will, I think, make you feel better."

She was tempted—so very tempted—to say what he wanted to hear, but it was too soon. There was too much to consider.

"I know you're worried about Luke," he said. "And a lot of other stuff..."

"Yes," she admitted, for as much as she wanted to, she couldn't forget what had happened during a season all those years ago—and how long it had taken her to get over it.

"What matters is you, Kate Harmon. And the fact that I love you. Nothing can change that."

In spite of her determination not to get excited about the future, Kate wanted to dance in circles and run through the fields shouting, "He loves me!" at the top of her lungs. Instead, she reined in her excitement and said in a calm voice, "After the season." He nodded, and when he kissed her this time, she felt the earth tremble.

CHAPTER NINE

OPENING DAY dawned clear and bright and perfect. Kate and her mother were in the sales stand shortly after six doing all the things they'd been too tired to do the night before—mainly because Kate had been running all over the field till dark picking what she called the monster berries for display. The four quarts she'd picked sat on the counter, every berry a brilliant red, and irresistible.

The stand was nestled between two enormous oak trees, which was heaven in the heat of summer, but sometimes a bit cool in the early mornings, and they were both shivering and gulping hot coffee while they worked.

Gladys came puffing up the driveway at six-thirty. "Good Lord, girls, the cars are lined up halfway to town." She put her lunch sack in the cooler. "Guess who's at the head of the pack?"

In unison, Kate and Sarah yelled, "Mrs. McChristian." Better known in the neighborhood as Miz Mac, she had to be pushing ninety, if not already on the downhill side. She drove a pale yellow Plymouth with enormous tail fins her husband had bought new in 1957. The neighbors called it Buttercup. She was the first customer every season. As soon as the gate opened, Miz Mac's Plymouth would come barreling down the drive, make a wide sweep near the strawberry field and skid to a stop, sometimes inches from the stand. They all had visions that one day the Plymouth would end up in the walk-in cooler, probably with one or more of them plastered to the monstrous chrome grill.

"You ladies take refuge behind the oak tree when I open the gate," Kate said, her tone more serious than joking.

Sarah frowned. "I can't believe she's still driving."

"Any fool can drive a car." Gladys snorted. "*I* can't believe she can stay on her knees all day in a strawberry field and then get up and walk. Lord, you'd have to hoist me up with the tractor boom." What Miz Mac did with the hundreds of pounds of strawberries she picked each year was a great mystery, but they assumed she just liked picking them and then probably gave most of them away. Kate had a number of older customers who did just that.

Several cars were waiting, and Kate gave a thumbs-up as she swung the gate open. Miz Mac spun her wheels, throwing gravel as she hurtled down the drive. Kate rode back in with one of her other customers in time to see a very shaken Jay retreating in the face of Miz Mac's sweeping turn. Gladys and Sarah yanked him to the safety of the oak tree. When the Plymouth came to a shuddering halt two feet from the stand, the tree contingent appeared again.

Miz Mac stood leaning on the counter. "Day's half-gone, girls. I been waitin' since sunup."

"Morning, Miz Mac," Kate said brightly.

The old woman picked an enormous berry out of one of the quart baskets. "Right puny this year, ain't they?"

Miz Mac started every season with the same words, and every season Kate responded with, "Yes'm, right puny."

"Gotta raise 'em on rocks, girl. Told you years ago these newfangled ways wouldn't amount to nothin'."

In the old days, farmers had raised strawberries on the flintrock hillsides, abandoning a field after two or three years and clearing a new hillside. The old-timers scoffed when she first planted strawberries in raised beds on flat ground, but few, with the notable exception of Miz Mac, scoffed anymore. "No, ma'am. How many buckets?"

"Gettin' started this late, four's all I have time for." Miz Mac waddled off to the field.

"What was *that*?" Jay said in a hushed tone.

"Miz Mac," they all whispered in unison. Sarah touched Jay's arm and told him that any time he saw Buttercup on the road, he was to take to the ditch at once.

Gladys and Sarah were chatting with customers, passing out buckets and generally having a wonderful time. Jay smiled at the quarts of strawberries. "Very impressive."

Kate waved a noncommittal hand. "Field-run berries."

Gladys burst out laughing. "'Field run' is when Kate runs all over the field searching out the biggest ones." She snatched up a monster berry and handed it to him. He took a bite, chewed, swallowed, took another bite and frowned.

"Well," Gladys demanded, "tell me you ever ate a California berry that tasted like that."

Jay took another bite, chewing thoughtfully. "Never have."

Gladys munched on a berry. "There's nothing like an Arkansas strawberry. It's like going to heaven."

"I hope Hector gets here today," Kate interjected. Hector Chavez and his family came up from south Texas for the strawberry harvest. Other Mexican families would come for the blueberry harvest. "Any chance you speak Spanish?" she said to Jay.

"You ask a farmer from California whether he speaks Spanish?" He said something in rapid-fire Spanish.

Kate caught only part of it, but it had to do with her *lack* of Spanish. "I know, it's on my list of things to do one winter. I speak a little, and most of the families have some English, so we get along, but every year I feel guilty because I haven't gotten better." Three more cars drove up and Kate put on her big straw hat. "I should get out in the field and start directing traffic."

She divided the field into ten sections and let customers pick two sections each day. That way, she started every morning with plenty of ripe berries. But customers sometimes wandered or didn't pick a row clean, so she spent most of the season in the field, directing customers to the best berries.

Jay touched her shoulder, saying he would see her later. "Your dad is going to explain the finer points of some of his machinery today. Feel like a burger tonight?"

"Not with Gladys and Mom running in and out of the kitchen cooking from now till we close. You're invited."

The day passed quickly, and when Kate at last sat down under the oak tree in late afternoon to eat a sandwich, Sarah told her it had been a crackerjack first picking. "Maybe a ton."

Kate was ecstatic. At that rate, she was looking at over fifteen thousand pounds of fruit per acre. As she chewed, Jay and Leonard appeared, covered in grease and oil. Jay was wiping his hands and shaking his head; Leonard was having the time of his life. "He's a mechanical genius," Jay told Kate, "but damned if I understand how some of it can work. It shouldn't. It's all baling wire and bubble gum."

Leonard grinned. "But it does, doesn't it?"

Jay nodded, then shook his head some more. Sarah pointed out that if they thought they were going to eat supper in her house looking like that they had another think coming. Leonard started to argue, but finally announced that he and Jay were going to town to lay in a supply of baling wire and bubble gum.

Kate slumped in her chair. It had been the usual hectic opening day, with a constant stream of people and hordes of kids who tried to eat their weight in berries—which she encouraged, knowing they were future customers. Kids who didn't want to eat and pick crowded into a nearby sandbox she kept well equipped with trucks and buckets and shovels.

She luxuriated in the few minutes of peace and quiet before the after-work rush arrived, and let her thoughts drift to Jay. She'd been sure it would take at least the strawberry season to see if he and her dad would get along, but here they were working together like old hands. And Kate realized she couldn't imagine the farm without Jay. If they made it through blueberries, she thought there was a good chance he might just stay in Arkansas. But if he had to go back to California, could she pick up and go? She'd hate to leave her farm, but she thought she probably could. *If* they made it through blueberries. Although she didn't think there was a chance in a million that he'd fold, she wasn't going to make any plans just yet.

She didn't bother to get up when a woman and small boy came toward her. The woman was in her late thirties, very attractive, and had what Kate always thought of as the well-groomed look of the city. The boy was five or six and clearly mad at the world.

When it was evident the woman wasn't sure where she should go, Kate pointed at the stand. "They'll take care of you over there."

The woman scrutinized her closely. "You must be Kate."

Kate stood up, brushing the crumbs off her T-shirt. "Yes. Can I help you?"

"You're exactly what I expected." The woman smiled. "I'm Beth, and this is Luke."

Kate ran through the card file in her head, trying to place them. Nothing surfaced, but it was hard to keep up with the names and faces of the hundreds of people who came to the farm each year. "Hi."

The boy scowled at her. "My name's William."

The woman rolled her eyes. "We've been through that for the last thousand miles. William is a fine name, but you've been Luke ever since I've known you."

Kate thought the woman was more than a little annoyed with her son, and judging from his expression, she could understand why. What on earth could make a little boy that sullen?

The woman looked out over the crowd in the fields. "How silly of me. You have legions of people this time of the year and you're expected to know every one of them by name, right?'' She extended her hand. ''I'm Jay's sister.''

Kate smiled and went to shake her hand, studying the boy with new eyes. ''And this is Jay's Luke. Good grief, he could have told us you were coming.''

Beth made a face. ''He didn't know. Luke got out of school a couple of weeks early, and I've been worried sick about Jay. He keeps telling me he's fine, but I wanted to see for myself, so I thought I'd bring Luke on out.''

''He'll be thrilled,'' Kate said. ''He's in town with my dad, but they won't be long. Can I get you some tea or juice or something?''

Beth waved off the offer. ''Just some room to stretch. It was a long trip.'' She looked at Kate more closely. ''I've been dying to meet you and see this place. My baby brother is hard to impress. And this farm is all Dad's talked about since the stroke. He's wild to get out here and oversee the harvest.''

Kate smiled and nodded as her mind raced, trying to shift gears and figure out what Beth was talking about. Her dad had to be Jay's dad. A stroke . . . and wanted to oversee the harvest . . . A sudden awful suspicion swept over her and she managed to ask, ''How's your dad doing?''

''Improved enough to drive us all crazy. I left him with his sister for a few days, so he could drive her up the wall for a change.''

Kate was amazed that her voice stayed so calm. ''When's he coming out?''

''I don't know. He should be well enough to travel soon, but as for ever running a farm? I doubt it.'' Then she smiled. ''Who can tell, though? Luther

Thomas is a man full of surprises. But I guess you already know that, don't you?''

Kate stared at Beth, unable to speak, desperately trying to rearrange Beth's words so they came out differently. Luther was Jay's father? That meant . . . it meant . . . the farm manager she'd been dealing with all these months was, in fact, the owner's son. Or probably part owner.

More to the point, it meant he had been here all these months looking after the family business.

Beth's hand went to a gold chain around her neck. "Good heavens," she said quietly. "He hasn't told you, has he?"

Kate shook her head, trying to fight back the tears welling in her eyes. "Just about Luke."

"*Damn* him, anyway." Beth groaned. "Well, I certainly brought more of a surprise than I ever intended. Oh, Kate, I'm sorry. So help me, I'll wring his neck."

"I'm sure he had his reasons," Kate said in a tight voice, although she couldn't think of any possible excuse for what he'd done. "If you'll excuse me, I really need to get back to the field."

Beth put a hand on Kate's arm. "He obviously got himself into something and didn't know how to get out again. Don't be too hard on him."

"Don't be too hard on him?" Kate muttered as she almost ran to the field. She was numb, trying to take it all in, trying to justify what he had done before she had to face him.

One part of her brain told her it was all a colossal mistake, a comedy of errors, that he loved her and that was all that mattered. Another part of her brain, the part tied to her heart, tried to stave off the pain—an ache that threatened to make her physically ill. Jay had come to Arkansas to protect his father's investment. He didn't trust Luther's faith in her. He didn't trust her to do right by Luther. But surely it hadn't taken him three months to see that she took care of Luther's farm just as she took care of her own.

He could have told her a hundred times. That night in the strawberry field, that time he told her about Luke, the evening on the bluff. He'd had all sorts of opportunities!

She retreated to the far end of the field, attacking the few weeds that had escaped her last sweep. As she yanked out crabgrass and nutsedge, she ran through the reasons that might account for his behavior. His divorce had made him leery of women. He had come to Arkansas to escape the hurt and because he didn't trust the people who'd sold his father a farm. Didn't trust the woman to whom a stroke-incapacitated father was sending thousands of dollars. He'd read her letters to Luther, written those terse notes and come out here to see why she hadn't hired someone.

She thought back to that day in February. Of course. He'd never asked about the job. She'd been the one who assumed he was looking for work. As the scene replayed in her mind, she realized that he had started to tell her something two or three times. But she had babbled on, distracted by his looks, practically forcing the job on him. And in the end, he'd said nothing. He had taken the job in order to watch her, to protect his father's investment. He'd probably hoped to discredit her so Luther would agree to sell the place.

All that made sense to Kate. It was what had come after those first weeks that didn't. *After* she'd started falling in love with him. He knew damn well she was losing her heart, so why hadn't he told her the truth? The only answer she could come up with was that he still hadn't trusted her, still felt a need to watch. And the whole time that she was making a fool of herself, melting with his kisses, he was . . . taking care of business. Which meant, of course, that he'd never intended to stay. He was probably just getting the place ready to sell so he could hightail it home. *But he loves you,* a voice insisted.

"Shut up," she muttered to a jimsonweed. "Oh, I suppose he was going to stick around for the harvest. *Then* take the loot and hightail it home. Stop at the first realtor's on the way and list the place, no doubt." She threw the jimsonweed as far as she could. While she'd been worrying about whether he'd *make* it through the harvest, he'd no doubt been worrying about making a good profit so the place would sell more easily. Since he practically owned the farm, of course he'd make it through the season—but for all the wrong reasons—at least in her mind.

When she stood up to stretch her back, she saw Luke walking down the field. Watching him, she decided "stomping" might be a more apt description. He was walking right down the middle of a row, stomping on plants and berries as hard as he could. He had all the appearance of an insufferable brat, which surprised and disappointed her. But he was not going to be a brat in her field.

"Young man," she yelled, "you get off those berries right this minute! Walk between the rows."

The boy stopped and looked at her, then raised his foot, bringing it down on a particularly big cluster of berries. "You can't tell me what to do!" he hollered.

"When you're in my field I can and I will. Or I'll pick you up by the scruff of the neck and throw you out."

His lower lip quivered. "My daddy owns this place."

"Your daddy owns that place," she said, pointing toward the big farm. "*I* own this place, and kids are welcome only when they know how to behave."

The boy kicked at the ground, but he did step off the row. As he came closer he said, "This is a stupid place. I hate it."

"So go back to California."

"My mom told me I'd hate it here. All the other guys went to camp."

In spite of herself, Kate was drawn to the pain in his voice. He was like a pup dropped by the side of the road, without the first notion of what he was doing there, except that some grown-up had done it. "What do they do at camp?"

"Swim and play soccer and make things." Suddenly Chester came loping down the field—being careful to stay between the rows after years of being yelled at—and butted Luke in the seat of the pants. The boy almost fell, but caught himself in time. He looked at the Lab, his face a mix of fear and anger. "Go away!"

"He lives here," Kate said.

"Dogs are dirty."

"Chester is clean. He's also nice." She went back to her weeds. When she glanced up again, Luke had squatted down in the row and was watching the dog. Chester panted and drooled and held up his paw to the boy, unable to imagine any human being on the face of the earth not loving him.

When she glanced that way again, Jay was striding down the field. She kept pulling weeds.

The next time she looked up, she was staring at his knees. "I'm busy."

He started to pull her to her feet, then stepped back, rubbing the back of his neck. "I've really screwed this one up, haven't I?"

She stood. "Yeah, I think you have. Got any other surprises up your sleeve? One month it's a son, the next, you own the place."

"I don't own it," he growled. "Dad does."

"Same difference."

"I was going to tell you after the harvest. I figured it wouldn't matter by then. I had no idea my dear sweet sister was planning a surprise." He looked at her for a long silent moment. "Dammit, it's not what you're thinking."

"How do you know what I'm thinking?"

"It's pretty obvious from the expression on your face. I didn't mean to fall in love, Kate," he said softly. "By the time it happened, I didn't know how to tell you. You were so damned gun-shy. I wanted you to love me enough that when the time came, it wouldn't matter."

"You lied to me." The fire she'd intended to put in her words came out as pain.

"I never lied to you," he said, his voice rising as his control wavered. "I just left out some of the truth."

"Same thing," she said, her voice rising to match his. "You thought I was trying to rip off Luther. You came here to spy on me."

The vein on his forehead stood out, and he took several deep breaths. "That's how it started, but it changed."

Her anger poured out in a flood of words. "Then that's when you should have told me, dammit! You hire on looking for all the world like a drifter, you let me make a fool of myself paying you minimum wage to work *my* strawberries because I thought you might need the money. You—"

"I hired on because the pull of this place, of you, touched something in me I thought was dead." His voice had dropped to a deadly softness, but his eyes flashed fire.

"You could just as easily have told me you were Luther's son, come to take over."

He began to pace. "You think I don't know that now?" He sucked in a great lungful of air and exhaled it slowly. "I couldn't believe you were all Dad said you were. I thought you'd be more honest with a drifter."

"You didn't trust me. Oh, you'd sleep with me, but you didn't trust me to handle your father's business." Even as the hurt spilled out, she didn't believe what she was saying, but she couldn't stop. "Were you waiting to see if I was going to skim off some of your harvest profits?"

"If you think that, you don't know me at all." He started toward her. "You think my love for you is a lie?"

"I don't know. I don't know anything anymore." Out of the corner of her eye, she saw Luke stomping on berries again. "Get off those berries, young man. Now!"

Jay looked toward his son. "Don't take it out on him. He's just a child."

"He's old enough to walk, he's old enough to respect my plants. Now, why don't you and your son go back to *your* farm?"

"You've got every right to be angry, but I thought this would help. You can't seem to love me because you're so damned worried that I don't belong here, that my ties are out West." He stood, hands jammed in his pockets, looking at her. "What greater tie could I have than my father living here?"

"But he's not living here, and you know as well as I do a man who's had a stroke will never run a farm this size."

"No, but dammit, I can run it for him!"

She looked at Luke, who was thrashing the air with a weed stalk as if he would annihilate the world. "And what about him? Is Luther's care and happiness more important than Luke's?" she said quietly, her anger suddenly spent.

"I can take care of both of them." He walked over, scooping up his son and giving Kate one last look. "When you've calmed down, we'll finish this."

"Don't hold your breath waiting."

Luke was struggling to get down, but Jay held him tightly and started out of the field. "It's okay, Luke. There's a really neat airport in town. You want to see some World War Two fighters?"

"I want my mother!" the boy shrieked, pounding on Jay's chest. "You promised you'd come on my birthday." Jay held him close and talked to him as they left the field.

In spite of her own pain, Kate's heart went out to father and son. Doubtless the boy had adored his father before the divorce. But how can a child understand why the person he loves most abandons him?

She went back to her weeds and stayed there the rest of the afternoon. When she finally came out of the field, her mother was waiting.

Kate accepted her mother's hug. "I suppose everybody in the world knows."

"Knows what, honey? That young people sometimes do foolish things and hurt each other? Everybody already knew that."

Kate reached down to brush dirt off her legs. "You know what I mean. I'm sorry about dinner tonight."

Sarah took her daughter by the arm and led her toward the house. "We're not canceling dinner, Katherine Ann Harmon. We're all stuck with each other for the season, so we might as well work it out right now."

Kate froze in her tracks. "I refuse to sit at the same table with him."

"Then you can eat outside. Gladys and I have worked too hard to have our dinner ruined by a spat. A good meal will do wonders."

Kate sighed. "Food won't cure this." But the more she worried, the more certain she was that Jay wouldn't show up. At least that was something to be grateful for.

"Maybe not, but it's a start. And in case you didn't notice, that little boy needs all the help he can get right now. Remember that scrawny pup you brought home when you were ten?"

"Mom..." Kate began, but before she could remind her mother they weren't talking about a puppy, Hector and his family drove in. She was glad to see them, but the timing could have been better. She pushed her own problems aside and forced a smile.

Hector got out of the truck shaking a finger at Kate. "You start without us, Kate?" Maria jumped out and stretched, and the three children climbed out of the camper.

"Just a trial run, Hector. *Como esta, amigo?*"

He tipped his hat at Sarah and replied that he was very well.

Kate hugged Maria, then gazed at the children. "What is this?" she exclaimed. "You trade in those little kids you had last summer for these big ones?" The children flashed smiles and shuffled their feet. They were always shy on the first day, but that would be gone by tomorrow.

"The little ones wouldn't work," Hector said. "These don't work, I trade them off for even bigger ones."

"We'll try them tomorrow," Kate said, ruffling the hair of the youngest child. "Your place is all ready." She turned to Maria. "Mom even put up new curtains this week." As she nodded in the direction of the trailers, she caught sight of Jay and her father coming toward them.

"Gracias." Hector waved and called to Leonard, "You look much better this year, *señor*. I always told you to winter in the south. Warm weather, warm water..."

Leonard shook hands and grunted, "Cold Republicans, Hector. No more south for me."

"Wrong south, *señor*. Come home with me this winter."

"I'm not figuring on going south again, but if I do, it'll be in your direction," Leonard said with a meaningful look at Sarah. "Still as pretty as ever, Maria."

Maria smiled and thanked him. Kate smiled and nodded and wondered how she could stand around visiting when her life was coming apart at the seams.

"*Gracias* to you for coming," she finally said, hoping everyone would go away. When the family drove off to their temporary home, she dropped her head and started toward the house, but Jay's voice stopped her.

"No wonder the same families come back every year. Too bad you don't treat all your workers with that much dignity."

She was pulled around by the raw anger in his voice. "You have a complaint?"

"Yeah," he said tightly.

She glared at him. "If you don't like it, the road that brought you here runs both ways." She felt the laser heat of his eyes, but refused to look away.

"You'd like that, wouldn't you?"

She smiled grimly. "Somehow I doubt you'll walk away from a crop like this. It wouldn't be good business, and that's what matters to you, isn't it?" She turned and started to walk off.

He grabbed her and pulled her close, his breath warm on her neck. "Can you walk away from this, Kate?" His kisses burned a fiery path down her neck. "You feel the same thing I do, Kate Harmon, and I'm not going to let you forget it."

She struggled to keep the fire at bay. "What I feel right now is hot and tired." She broke out of his arms and turned to face him. Anger flashed in his eyes.

"What you *feel*," he whispered, "is a hunger that burns in your belly like a prairie fire in August. And it scares the hell out of you. Well, it scares the hell out of me, too."

The quickness of his perception rocked her. "Go away."

"Oh, no, dear Kate, I don't intend to make it that easy for you."

"Then go tend your farm. You've got a big investment to take care of."

Kate was vaguely aware of her parents fussing somewhere nearby. "Who in the hell put burrs under their saddles?" Leonard asked in a loud whisper as Sarah hustled him off toward the house.

"Never mind, Leonard. It's none of your business."

"Everything on this place is my business, woman."

"Well, this *isn't,* old man."

"It's not the crop that will keep me here, Kate," Jay said through clenched teeth. "And you have to deal with me sooner or later. I have the equipment."

"And I have the water," she said, wrenching herself away from the force of his anger—and the fiery depths of his eyes.

CHAPTER TEN

WHEN KATE CAME DOWNSTAIRS after her shower, she was relieved to find her father napping, her mother in the kitchen and no guests, not even Gladys. Her relief was short-lived, however, when ten minutes later Gladys arrived, herding an objecting Beth, a wire-tense Jay and a sullen Luke. Gladys looked for all the world like a mother hen gathering her batch of reluctant chicks for the night.

Kate was tempted to make a U-turn back up the stairs and take to her bed, but it was her house and why should she be run out? Besides, it looked as if Jay might be *very* busy with his son tonight. Too busy to annoy her.

As she began clearing the big oak table in the living room, she tried to figure out a seating arrangement that would get her the farthest away from Jay—which was difficult with a round table. And which was a waste of time since Gladys had her own arrangement in mind, an arrangement that put Kate directly across from Jay.

"This looks wonderful," Beth said, fixing plates for herself and Luke.

"I don't want any of that," Luke whined. "It's yucky and greasy." He sat slumped down in his chair, his skinny arms crossed over his chest, hands balled into fists.

A flush began on Jay's neck. "These ladies worked very hard on this meal, son. You—"

"Jay," Beth warned, obviously having been down this road before. "You love mashed potatoes, Luke."

"That gravy's white," Luke complained. "Gravy's s'posed to be brown."

Kate picked at a chicken leg, thinking it was going to be a long meal. She didn't want to feel sorry for Jay's son, didn't want to feel his pain, but she couldn't help herself.

Luke glared defiantly at his father and then his aunt. "Only stupid people eat greasy stuff."

Before Jay or Beth could respond, Gladys nudged Sarah. "Sarah, did you hear about the little Brashears boy?"

"Not a word. He must be about six by now."

"Going on seven," Gladys said in a somber voice. "And rigid as a board. They carry him out on the porch afternoons to take some sun. Prop him up like a stick of wood."

"No," Sarah said, her hand to her breast.

Kate glanced at Luke. In spite of his best efforts to despise everything and everyone, Gladys had hooked him. Beth and Jay looked bewildered by the sudden turn of events.

"Some kind of disease?" Beth asked.

"Oh, no, my dear," Gladys said in hushed tones. "His parents were health-food, no-fat people. Fanatics, really. Something called tofu, I believe. Such a shame."

The flush on Jay's neck spread to his face. "He'll eat when he gets hungry. There's no need to—"

Leonard waved Jay quiet and shook a drumstick at Luke. "Let's see if you can pop your knuckles, boy."

The boy shot a quick look at his aunt, then laced his fingers and bent them backward, pleased to demonstrate a skill that usually got him yelled at. One loud pop and a few crunching sounds brought the first sign of a smile to his face. Leonard nodded at Gladys. "No doubt about it, he'll freeze up like a dried-out gear one of these days. You need a grease job, boy." He wiggled his fingers and reached for the gravy. "Nothing like gravy for keeping a man limber."

Sarah and Gladys laced their fingers together and put their hands through all sorts of gyrations, but couldn't produce a pop between them. "Such a shame," Gladys said, and resumed eating.

Kate bent to her food, watching Luke out of the corner of her eye. Gladys's tale was an outrageous one to tell a child, but she could almost hear the wheels turning in the boy's head, feel him waiting for someone to tell him he would end up like the nonexistent Brashears boy. But nobody did, and it occurred to her that what Luke needed now was a way to save face. She glanced at Jay, who was seething. She got the impression that Beth was kicking him under the table to keep him from expressing an opinion about this particular method of child-rearing. "I just remembered a show I wanted to watch," she said brightly. "Anybody interested?"

There were no takers as Kate picked up her plate and moved to the sofa. She found a really awful sitcom that appeared to have a mental rating of about five, and she settled in to suffer through it. Within minutes, Luke brought his plate to the couch, too, and crawled up on the sofa. When she figured he was hooked, she eased back to the table.

No one could see Luke over the back of the sofa, but they could hear the encouraging sounds of eating. Beth was trying hard not to laugh. "Prop him up on the porch to take the sun? I'll bet Dr. Spock never heard that one."

"He needs time to adjust to a new diet," Jay said in a tight voice. "I don't think scaring and—"

"Nonsense, dear," Gladys said, and patted his arm. "A little meat on his bones will make him feel better. Now you musn't put too much stock in all those books. Puppies and boys have so much in common."

Kate suspected Jay's anger came from a mixture of embarrassment over the strain between him and his son, and fear that they'd found him wanting as a father. He'd better watch it, she thought, or Gladys and Sarah would adopt Luke permanently.

While they were cleaning up, Luke appeared with an empty plate. "Those stupid dogs ate it," he said, refusing to look at anyone.

Kate took his plate. "They're real bad about that." When he went back to the television, Beth sighed.

"I think I'm glad I'm going home in a few days."

Gladys patted her shoulder. "All that child needs is a good letting alone for a bit. Sun, fresh air and home cooking will do wonders."

"I hope you're right. I think both Jay and Luke are real lucky to have all of you to help them."

Sarah deftly changed the subject. She asked Beth about California and if she'd ever considered living somewhere else, and no more was said about Luke and what the summer might be like.

As Kate put the clean dishes away, she couldn't help but wonder what her father and Jay were talking about, closeted in the study. Plotting about her, no doubt, she thought with a sigh.

While Beth roused Luke from his TV show and Gladys packed up food for them to take home, Jay cornered Kate by the front door. "I know how to take care of my son."

Kate flinched at the anger in his voice, but when she looked into his eyes, all she saw was pain. "No one said you didn't," she said quietly.

"I'll work this thing out, dammit."

She threw back the words he had said to her so often. "But wouldn't it be easier with help? Mom and Gladys have a lot of experience."

"Are you implying that I don't know what the hell I'm doing? Or that I've managed to screw up my kid so badly he's hopeless?"

She bristled. "You won't hear that from any of us, only from yourself. And what did you have in mind? Keeping Luke shut in that trailer all summer? Away from everyone? That ought to solve things."

"No. I... Forget it." He rubbed his forehead. "Come on, Beth," he yelled, and slammed out the door.

When they were gone, Sarah sent Leonard to bed and poured two mugs of coffee. "Let's go out on the porch," she said to Kate.

Kate took a mug. "Looks like a long hot summer ahead."

They sat, sipping coffee in silence. Finally Sarah chuckled and patted Kate's leg. "Did you know your father was promised to the youngest McChristian girl?"

Kate frowned. "Miz Mac's daughter?"

Sarah nodded. "Mr. Harmon had decided. Oh, my, was he fit to be tied when I set my cap for Leonard."

Kate was amazed she'd never heard this story before. "Was Daddy... you know..."

"In love with Ruth? No, but both families just expected it." She laughed. "Sort of like you and Barry. Dad Harmon was a man of great persuasive powers, kind of like a bulldog with something between his jaws."

"So what happened?"

"I wanted Leonard and I went out and got him right before he went into the army. Didn't give one whit whether anybody liked it or not."

Kate smiled. "And Daddy didn't have a clue about what was happening, right?"

"Well, maybe a clue, but I knew we were meant for each other the first time I set eyes on the old fool. 'Course, he wasn't an old fool then. He was young and strong and loved this land like he'd been hatched out of it."

Kate sighed. "And the moral of this story is?"

"No moral, honey. But I spent four years with him at a godforsaken army base in west Texas. Nothing but dust and rattlesnakes. Every day of that four years I wondered whether I'd have been so set on him if I'd known what was ahead."

"And?"

"I probably would have let him go alone and spent thirty-five years regretting it." She laughed. "Not to mention what your father might have gotten into that *he* would have sorely regretted." She leaned back. "Would you have done anything differently with Jay if you'd had all the information you have now?"

"I don't know. I just keep thinking of everything I've said and done, thinking I was dealing with some drifter, not Luther's son, not somebody who's managed farms that make this one look like a truck garden. And thinking he needed money." She heaved a great sigh.

"It's embarrassing, Mom. He must have been laughing his head off the whole time. And I can't stand the idea of anybody thinking I'd rip off that sweet old man."

"Which he probably thought for about two minutes."

"But I don't know that. I mean, he might have pretended to...you know...just so he could find out more about my business practices."

Sarah reached up and squeezed her daughter's hand. "You don't believe that."

"Maybe not. But I was all ready to follow him to the ends of the earth, and now I'm not even sure he wants me to. And there's the whole situation with Luke and whether Luther will ever come out here..."

"That poor little boy needs some good old-fashioned love. You think it through, honey, and think it through long and hard. Jay's a proud one."

Kate flared up. "Well, so am I."

THREE DAYS LATER Kate was, as usual, hiding in the fields worrying about Jay. She hadn't caught even a glimpse of him. According to all reports he and Leonard were up to their elbows in machinery. She'd seen Beth walking by the river, and she'd seen plenty of Luke, because he hung around the strawberry field and watched her. Every day he came a little closer, but he still wouldn't speak. At least he wasn't walking on the berries now. Chester had abandoned the boy as no fun at all, but Molly had taken over, trailing Luke everywhere, nuzzling him at every opportunity, nudging him here and there, as if she found this creature needed some mothering.

Kate, for her part, made no overtures, figuring that kids in pain were like animals in pain. They came to you when they were good and ready—when they were ready to trust.

In midmorning, she looked up to see Beth coming toward her. She regretted that she hadn't talked to Jay's sister since that first day. In other circumstances, she thought that the two of them would have been friends.

"I'm leaving," Beth said. "I'm sure that getting at least one Thomas out of your hair will be a relief."

"It's not your fault," Kate said, and meant it.

"Be that as it may, it's time to leave the two of them alone." She cocked an eyebrow at Kate. "And I guess the two of you, or the three."

In spite of her intention not to get involved any further with the Thomas family, Kate was worried about Luke. "How's it going?"

Beth shuddered. "Don't ask. Luke is so full of anger. And love. Jay is full of guilt. And love. And I keep getting caught in the middle. If I'm not here they'll have to work it out themselves." Beth looked over at Luke. "The trip out here was…difficult, to say the least."

"How can such a little boy be so angry?"

"You'd have to know Jennifer. Luke didn't get out of school early— She took him out early so she could flit off to Europe with her friends. I hope she meets some sleazy count who doesn't like children.

"However, to make a long story short, Jay and Luke were always inseparable. With the divorce, Luke lost his daddy and all his friends, since Jen didn't think farmers' and migrant workers' kids were a good influence. He was moved to San Francisco, put in a very expensive school full of very expensive brats and probably told on a daily basis how much his father doesn't love him. Jen doesn't want Luke as much as she wants to punish Jay for reducing her status from lady of the winery to wife of a farmer. And of course Jay lost the farm he loved in the property settlement."

"Good Lord."

"Yeah. Luke's a wonderful kid, although you'd never guess it now." Beth twisted the gold chain around her neck. "Kate, what Jay did was outrageous. But he was so bitter, so hurt when he left California. You can't imagine." She held up her hand when Kate started to say something. "I know, it doesn't excuse anything, but he needed some time to heal, and he found it on this farm. Hard work, growing things, and a woman who was exactly what she seemed. Believe me, Kate, falling in love was not on his agenda for the next hundred years or so. But once he did, the big lug, he didn't know how to tell you who he was. I'm sure he had visions of you ordering him off the place and never wanting to see him again. The Thomas men are too damn proud for their own good."

Kate smiled slightly and reached out to touch Beth's arm. "Thanks for telling me this, Beth. I needed to know."

"He's a good man, Kate. But he won't come begging."

"I don't want begging, I just want him to tell me what you've told me."

Beth looked at Kate doubtfully. "Did you give him the chance?"

Kate shrugged, thinking of the awful things she'd said to Jay, things that were hard to take back. "It'll be a few weeks before I can do anything about it. I don't have the energy to get through a harvest and sort out my life all at the same time."

Beth gave her a quick hug. "You're everything Dad said you were, Kate. If it looks like those two are going to kill each other, give me a call." She started to move away, then turned.

"He hasn't said anything to me, but if I know my brother, he either won't say a word till you do or he'll bully you unmercifully. Be prepared for either one."

Kate watched Beth walk back to the parking area, saw Luke cling to her for long moments, then stand and watch her car drive away. She could tell even from this distance that the boy's chest heaved with sobbing and the tears streamed down his face. Molly sat beside him, jumping up from time to time to lick his tears. The boy tried his best to get her to go away. He pounded her broad back and yelled at her, but she stayed with him, kept licking his tears until Jay came and carried him off. By that time Kate was almost in tears herself.

In the middle of the afternoon, Kate looked up to see Luke standing at the edge of the field, twiddling Molly's ears. She ignored them and half an hour later, she noticed Luke trailing behind her, closer than before, watching her intently. She wandered over to where Hector and his family were picking for the stand.

Hector sat back on his heels, wiping his face with a bright bandanna. "I been coming here how many years now? I never see berries like this."

"We did good this year, didn't we?"

"*Muy bueno.*"

She nodded toward Luke. "Too bad we don't have more pickers, Hector. I don't think you guys are going to be able to handle it."

"*Si.* Is a lot of berries for us. Another good strong hand is what we need. You know any big strong boys?"

Kate shook her head. "Sure don't. A shame, isn't it?"

Hector and Marie's youngest child, a boy of about eight, had gone over to Luke. Luke spoke to him in rapid Spanish. Smiling, Hector winked at Kate. "Hey, boy," he said in Spanish. "You think you're big enough to work?"

Luke looked at Kate for a long moment, then nodded.

"Get some quarts and I show you how to pick."

Luke kicked at a plant. "I know how to pick."

"You *think* you know." Hector shook his finger. "But there's pickers and there's *pickers,* and I'm the best. You don't pick what Miss Kate wants, she fire us all."

"That's right," Kate said in her most serious voice. "I don't pay for trash or rot or green."

Luke frowned. "How much do you pay?"

"Going rate, a quarter a quart. We pay by the day or the week, however you want it. And I inspect every quart."

When Kate walked away, Luke was on his knees beside Hector, showing him every berry before it went

into his basket. It was the first time she'd seen the boy
smile since he'd arrived. She made a mental note to
add some quarts to Hector's daily total to make up for
his time and trouble.

When she got back to the pick-your-own part of the
field, Jay was there, helping customers pick berries,
handing out extra buckets, generally making himself
useful. Kate waited until there was a lull to say anything. "I don't need any help out here."

"I know. So tell me what you want me to do."

"Nothing."

"You hired me for the strawberry season, remember?"

"That was before..."

"Before what, Kate?" His voice flicked at her like
a whip.

"Before I found out you couldn't possibly need the
money."

"It was a verbal contract. Binding."

Kate rolled her eyes. "Oh, go away."

He crossed two rows in one jump. "No, Kate, I will
not go away."

She started for the shed. "Then I will."

But he caught her by the arm. "You can tell me
what needs doing and pay me, or I can spend the season right here," he said softly, "helping you."

"No, you can't!" she snapped. "This is absurd.
Ridiculous. Outrageous."

"Your call." He pushed her straw hat back until he
could see her eyes. "Am I so different from what I was
a few days ago? Have all those feelings just gone
away?" He stroked her cheek, watching the flush
spread. "I didn't think so."

"Go away," she said, hearing the lack of conviction.

"Sooner or later you have to deal with your feelings, Kate." He brushed her cheek with a kiss. "And sooner or later you have to deal with me."

Before she could argue he was striding away. "Beth said you were a bully," she yelled after him.

That evening, Luke proudly handed over his picker's card with six quarts punched. He had strawberry-juice handprints all over his expensive yellow T-shirt and his knees were filthy. Kate thought it was a good sign as she solemnly counted out his dollar and a half. Coming from obvious affluence, she was afraid he might throw a tantrum at such a pittance, but he was all smiles and stuffed the money into the pockets of his shorts, telling her he would pick ten quarts the next day.

"You'll be up to twenty or thirty quarts a day before you know it," she said.

He screwed up his face and studied Kate. "Are you the hillbilly hussy my dad's drooling over?"

Kate didn't know whether to laugh or cry. Sarah, who was watching the exchange, had to go to the cooler. "Do I look like a hillbilly or a hussy, Luke?"

"I don't know," the boy said, kicking at the dirt with the toe of one sneaker. "I don't know what those words mean."

"Well, have you noticed any drool on your dad's chin?" The boy shook his head.

"Then somebody was probably pulling your leg. You know what that means?"

Luke nodded. "It's a story that's not true."

"You got it. Now go wash up." She sent him on his way with a pat, and when she looked up, she saw Jay leaning against the oak tree, staring at her. He was beginning to remind her of Snit, ready to pounce. And *she* was beginning to feel like the mouse.

THE STRAWBERRY SEASON rushed by in a blur of people and berries, of warm dry days, the kind of season growers dream of but hardly ever get. Long days and short nights. Kate had finally put Jay in charge of delivering berries to the stores. It was either that or put up with him hanging around either looking gloomy or bullying her.

By the third week, the berries peaked. The size dropped, but the fruit was still gorgeous and they had more customers than they could handle. Mentally Kate began to shift gears from strawberries to the rapidly approaching blueberry harvest. Sometimes she got lucky and had a week between crops. As she wandered through the ripening blueberries, she knew they would probably be picking both crops at once this year.

"Call in the end-of-the-year special, Mom," she said when she got back to the stand. At the end of the season she ran a strawberry-jam special, hoping to get the fields stripped before blueberries. Gladys and Sarah protested that it wasn't time, that the berries were still lovely. "Yeah, but those stupid blueberries are turning. I've got to get some bird balloons up. Tell customers the far end looks good."

She went to the shed to pull out the yellow balloons that theoretically kept birds out of the fields. She didn't think they worked, but they made her feel better. When she walked into the shed, Jay was working on the bird cannons, the timed explosions of which were also designed to keep birds out. He looked up, his face glistening with sweat. "Your dad said it was time for these."

"It is. I came to get the balloons ready." She rummaged on a storage shelf and pulled out several boxes. "Is the air compressor on?" she yelled.

"I'm not deaf," he said right behind her.

She jumped. "Will you quit sneaking up on me?"

He blocked her exit. "It's the only way I can get you alone. You want some help hanging these?"

"I'll get some of the kids. Do you know how to set up the cannons?"

"Your dad's going to help." When she started past him, he seized her by the shoulders. "Dammit, Kate, talk to me."

She tried to wrench away, but he held her tight. "I thought we *were* talking," she growled.

"Balloons and cannons, sure, but who the hell cares? I feel like I'm alone in a crowd of people. You don't talk, Luke doesn't talk—except to you and Sarah." He pulled her close and kissed her. "Talk to me, Kate. Now."

Her hands trembled as she pushed against his chest. "Balloons and cannons is all I *can* talk about right now. I'm tired. I'm not ready for the blues. I...I thought after the season..."

He threw a box of balloons across the shed. "Is one stupid season more important than the rest of your life?"

The ghost of another season reared its ugly head and Kate swallowed hard. "The season *is* my life right now. Surely you understand that."

"What I understand is that I'm not of much use to anyone except as a field grunt, and you can get all of them you need at the employment office."

She flinched at words that were all too familiar. "That's not fair and you know it." *Dear Lord,* she thought, *don't let this be happening. We're not even into the main harvest yet.* "We made a deal," she said softly. "After the season. And Luke's getting better."

"With everyone but me."

She took a deep breath. "Jay, you may have to go through this every summer as long as you're apart."

He turned away and snatched up another box. "I'll get the kids to inflate these."

An hour later, Kate and Luke and Hector's kids were hanging the bright yellow balloons.

"Why do these scare the birds?" Luke asked, handing her a string.

"See the big hawk eyes on each side? The birds think the field is full of giant hawks ready to gobble them up."

The kids all giggled. "A hawk with eyes that big would be as big as an airplane," Luke scoffed. "Are the birds that stupid?"

She tied the balloon in place. "Probably not. We're going to need more string, gang." Hector's kids tore off for the shed. She and Luke worked in silence for a few minutes, until she decided this was as good a time as any to talk to him. "So how do you like this place now?"

He shrugged. "It's okay." He looked up and grinned. "It's kinda fun. You think I could stay here?"

She gulped. "Probably not, but you could come for lots of visits. Didn't I once hear you say that this place was stupid?"

"Yeah."

When he fell silent she pressed on. "So how are you and your dad making out?"

"Okay, I guess. Are you and him getting married?"

"I don't know. You think we should?"

He shrugged. "I guess if you did you'd have your own kid and wouldn't want me."

She moved close and hugged him. "Luke Thomas, don't you ever say that again. You hear me?" She lifted his chin and made him look at her. "Now where did you get an idea like that?"

He looked abashed. "I heard it. Around."

"Well, it's not true. If I had to choose a kid from all the kids in the world, you know who I'd choose?" He looked up, his lower lip quivering, and shook his head. "You," she growled, "because you're a good field hand."

His lip still quivered. "You're just saying that."

She shook her head and took a red felt marking pen out of her pocket. She drew a huge X across the front of her T-shirt. "Cross my heart and hope to die, stick a needle in my eye," she said solemnly.

His eyes got big. "Mom would kill me if I did that."

"Well, what are T-shirts for?" she demanded. "Now, short lecture. Your dad is miserable because he loves you so much and he thinks you don't love him even a little bit. He didn't go see you on your birthday so he could see you more later. Grown-ups screw up a lot and sometimes kids have to pay." She drew another X on her shirt. "Truth, cross my heart. Your dad needs you right now, Luke. You love him?"

He dropped his head and nodded.

"Promise to tell him that? And to talk to him about what makes you sad?" The boy nodded again. "Okay, promise. Cross your heart and hope to die?'' He nod-ded and she solemnly drew an enormous red X on the front of his shirt.

Luke pulled his T-shirt away from his chest to ad-mire it. "If I promise both things," he said softly, "can I have two X's, too?"

"You got it," she said, and drew the second one.

CHAPTER ELEVEN

KATE SWIGGED tepid water from her thermos while the Sanchez men loaded flats of blueberries onto the truck. The harvest was almost over, but Kate wasn't sure she would make it through the next week or so. The harvest was exceeding even her wildest estimates. The weather had turned scorching and they were picking till early afternoon when the berries got too hot, then going back to the fields at seven and picking till dark. The packing line ran till the wee hours of the morning, the harvester had been going for two nights, and the strain was beginning to show on everyone.

She took off her straw hat and swiped at her forehead. She was picking up flats of berries for both farms, which she hadn't planned on, but everyone was working as many hours as he or she could stand. She didn't think Jay was even going to bed most nights. He was doing an incredible job, but there were still a lot of tasks he was unfamiliar with that she had to supervise. Which meant she saw him a lot, but there was no time to talk, no time for anything except an endless river of blueberries.

"Kate, the truck's loaded."

She shook herself and realized that Rose Sanchez was standing beside her. "You work too hard," the woman said. "You and the big man. What are you two trying to forget?"

"Nothing." Lord, did everyone in the world know about her and Jay?

"I see the way he looks at you. I see the way you *don't* look at him. *El fuego!*"

"No fire, just exhaustion."

The woman smiled. "The children would be beautiful!"

Kate jammed her hat back on her head. She wanted to get the season over with so she and Jay could at least talk. Now there were never even an extra few minutes.

Jay was working on one of the packing tables when she drove up. He'd turned several shades darker, and his sweat-soaked T-shirt clung like a second skin, outlining the hard flat muscles of his chest and stomach. Every time she saw him, her heart seemed to rocket into the vicinity of her throat.

A dozen women stood at the six packing tables, taking each pint from a field flat, putting cellophane and a rubber band over the top of the pint, placing it in the cardboard flat that would go to market. They were packing about four tons of berries a day, one pint at a time.

While the shed crew unloaded the truck, Kate filled her thermos and chatted with the women on the line before retiring to a quiet spot in the corner of the shed for a few minutes' rest.

"Do you have nightmares about blueberries, or is it just us first-timers?"

Kate jumped at the sound of Jay's voice. She turned to see him leaning against the wall, his arms crossed over his chest, just as he'd been leaning against the harvester that day so long ago. "You have to sleep to have nightmares," she said softly. "I don't remember doing much of that this year."

"I'm beginning to understand your statement that if two people can get through a harvest, they can get through anything."

She arched an eyebrow and smiled. "Yeah, and it looks like you're going to survive it."

"That was never a question—except for you." He wiped his face with a bandanna. "Does that mean I get a gold star? Or maybe a kiss from the farmer lady?"

"Too sweaty right now. Anyhow, you and Luther will do real well this year."

"You do have a knack for changing the subject, but yeah, Dad calls regularly. I told him last night I was drowning in a sea of blue. He sounded good." Jay smiled. "He wants to be here. Beth's threatening to tie him to a tree."

"I'm glad. Say hello to him for me."

"You okay?" His voice was husky.

She shrugged. "Counting the days till the end. You?"

"I wouldn't have made it without you and Leonard."

"I knew it was a great crop, but not *this* great." She put her hat on. "Guess I better get back to the fields."

"You ready to talk?"

She glanced around at the frantic activity. It was only a few more days, and she wanted someplace a little more romantic than the packing shed to declare her love. "Maybe, but not here, between loads." He smiled and she thought she might melt.

"Don't wait too long...."

He was still smiling, but his words had thrown her. He'd quit bullying her a couple of weeks ago—about the same time she'd noticed Luke hanging around him more. Then she'd seen them talking, Luke riding the harvester... She was delighted that they seemed to be back on track, but somewhere in the process Jay had pretty much quit confronting her. Which either meant he figured they'd work things out or he'd begun to understand what she'd been trying to tell him—that long separations spelled disaster, and that the only way to prevent long separations was for him to be near Luke.

Which meant what? Her train of thought was interrupted when Luke popped up beside the truck wearing his T-shirt with the red X's, now faded from many washings. "Swim, Kate? It's awful hot."

She ruffled his hair and stuck her head out the side door of the shed. The smaller kids were playing in the sandbox. "I might be persuaded to stop at the lake for ten minutes if I get some help with the next load," she said loudly. Almost before the words were out of her mouth, a dozen kids were scrambling onto the truck.

"Okay," she ordered, "no standing up, no horsing around. You know the drill." The kids were under strict orders not to go near the lake without adult supervision, but the days were long and hot, so when she could spare the time, Kate took them for a quick swim.

She pulled the truck up beside the lake and the kids scrambled off and into the water like a swarm of otters. She waded in with them, clothes and all.

They giggled, screaming that she wasn't supposed to swim in her clothes. She plunged into the delicious cool and played Nessie, grabbing at sturdy little legs beneath the water. More giggling, squealing and splashing. After a few minutes, she climbed out to dry off a bit before she went back to work, letting the kids entertain themselves. She watched them carefully, but her eyes kept drifting to Luke.

His transformation had been little short of miraculous. He had turned as brown as a nut in the Arkansas sun, and the browner he got, the more he acted like any other little kid. The Mexican women and children had pulled him into their circle, and he seemed to be having a great summer. As for her, she'd come to love the boy as much as she loved his father.

She shivered, not from the hot wind on her wet clothes, but with anticipation of the end of the season. A nagging voice told her she was being foolish to wait, crazy to hold out for that perfect private moment that wasn't possible right now, but she pushed the voice aside.

"Okay, gang," she yelled. "Time to get to work." There were groans, but everybody scrambled to the truck. She drove toward the nearest picking crew and the kids were off in a flash, scattering down the rows to carry buckets of berries back to pour into the flats.

The adults stopped their work for a few minutes to hoot, "*La patrona* plays in the water while we work."

"No choice," she said. "The natives were getting restless in the sandbox. They threatened *revolucion*."

"GLADYS IS BRINGING supper," Sarah informed her when she took a break before the evening picking started.

"I think I'm too tired to eat." Kate was sprawled under the oak tree, drinking cold orange juice.

"Honey, ease up. The big farm isn't your responsibility anymore."

"I know, but it's not fair to dump a harvest like this on Jay."

Sarah's eyebrows arched. "Now we're worried about Jay?"

"Not worried, exactly." There had been little opportunity even to speak to her mother in weeks, let alone really talk. When Sarah asked if she and Jay had things worked out, Kate shook her head. "No time."

"I'll rephrase the question. Have *you* got things straight in your head?"

Kate nodded, but before she could say more, Gladys drove in and began to unpack baskets. "I suppose, as usual, there's no time to sit down to a decent meal," the old woman said pointedly to Kate. "And it does absolutely no good to remind you how important one's digestion is in later life. And that it suffers gravely from the abuse of eating on the run."

Kate laughed. "Hi, Gladys."

"Don't 'Hi' me, young lady. You're all wasting away to nothing. Now Sarah, make sure Leonard goes to the house and eats at the table. It improves one's digestion." She lined up plates on the counter and glared at Kate. "And you go get the boys. Poor Jay, how could you?"

"What?"

"You know very well what. I suggest you get a grip."

Get a grip? Kate wiped the smile off her face and said, "Yes, ma'am."

"Don't be impertinent." Gladys went back to her car for another load.

Kate looked at her mother. "What was that all about?"

"She's afraid you're going to blow it."

"Blow it? Get a grip? She's got to quit listening to her grandson. Oh, well... Are you off to feed Daddy and make him rest?"

Sarah picked up two plates. "He's doing fine, honey. Jay keeps him occupied with repairs. Little repairs. Now you sit down and I'll call Jay. I think Luke went off with Hector and crew for supper."

Kate ate quickly, then lay down under the oak tree to catch a quick nap before the evening's work began. Molly and Chester, who felt somewhat neglected in the rush of the season, bounded over and flopped down beside her.

"You guys get away from me," she complained. "You're hot and furry." The dogs moved maybe two inches and settled in. "And don't breathe on me."

"That's what you looked like the first time I saw you."

Her eyes popped open and she saw Jay—upside down—just the way she'd seen him that first time. She tried to shake her weariness away. "I could stay here forever. Preferably without the dogs."

"I come over here for dinner conversation and you're having a snooze." He smiled and sat down, his back against the tree, letting the dogs have what was left of his meal. "Mmm, this does feel good."

She looked at his face and saw the lines of strain. She wondered if they were from the harvest or whether things with Luke were maybe not as good as they appeared. She realized, with a twinge of guilt, that they'd never really talked about his son. "How are things going with Luke?'' she said quietly, relishing this rare tranquil moment.

Jay's eyes closed and he rubbed Molly's chest. "Rocky at first, but getting better." He smiled. "I don't suppose you would know anything about the big red X's on his favorite T-shirt, would you?"

"Nope. Must be a secret club."

"Have anything to do with the ones on your shirt a few weeks ago?" When she denied all knowledge he continued, "After that we had some long talks, some longer shouting and crying spells, and then things got better. I think maybe I owe you a thanks." He threw her a sidelong glance. "He likes you. A lot."

She rolled over onto her stomach. "What will happen when he has to go back?"

"I don't know."

"How often can you see him?" She sensed a change in Jay. The anger was gone, replaced by something she couldn't identify.

"Depends on what the court says this fall."

She picked her words carefully. "If you were to, you know, stay here, you might have to go through this every summer."

His eyes flashed with the old familiar anger. "I'll worry about Luke. You worry about whether or not I'm going to stay."

Flinching at his tone, she tried to blame his words on exhaustion. But what if he wasn't sure in his own mind that he wanted to stay? Before she could respond, he rubbed his eyes with both hands. "Look, I'm tired and, as Leonard would say, gettin' real testy."

She reached over and put a hand on his knee. "Hang in there. We'll make it—"

Her words were interrupted when someone yelled for Jay from the door of the shed. "Jam up on the cooler line!"

Jay stood and stretched. "No rest for the weary." He looked at her for a long moment. "Luke keeps asking questions. We have to get on with our lives soon. One way or the other." He backed toward the shed. "I screwed up, Kate. Don't you do the same thing."

"Jay..." she called. She rose to go after him, tell him she wasn't about to let him go, when Barry's car tore into the yard. Her old friend was out and running before the dust cleared, swooping her up in his arms and swinging her around. As she struggled to free herself, she looked over Barry's shoulder. Jay was standing at the door of the shed watching, chewing his lip.

"Put me down, Barry, you're going to drop me."

Barry lowered her and bussed her cheek. "You do get cranky during harvest."

"You'd get cranky, too, if you were drowning in blueberries. Now, what was that all about?"

"Angie. We might be getting married. At least she didn't run off when I suggested it."

In spite of her exhaustion, Kate laughed. "That's what I call progress. Congratulations."

Barry swelled up to his best courtroom form. "So as of this moment, I release you from all vows of marriage spoken at age seven."

Kate curtsied. "And I release you from all those vows I never agreed to."

"Which means, dear Kate, that you are now free to marry your hired hand, who turned out to be Prince

Charming. You've come to your senses and forgiven all, haven't you?''

"Yeah, I guess so."

"Then why are you looking so miserable? And where is he? And why aren't you running off to somewhere exotic?''

"In case you hadn't noticed, Barry, the harvest has a way of taking the edge off romance. There'll be plenty of time in a couple of weeks. When I'm not so cranky."

"Good Lord, girl, you're letting that poor sap stew all this time?''

"Has Gladys told you someone's stewing?''

"The source is not the point. Do it, Kate," he said seriously, "before he gets away."

"He better not be going anywhere, not with all these damn berries. Now *I* have to get back to work."

"How can you think of work when love is in the air?''

"Sounds like a great song title. Goodbye, Barry."

"Kate . . ." he wailed.

She didn't see Jay again that day. One of the cooler compressors broke down, and they had a load due in Oklahoma City the next morning.

In the week that followed, Kate saw Jay only in passing. He was running the harvester at night, the freezer-pack line was in full swing, and they were picking the last of the fresh market berries. On Tuesday morning, Hector told her the crews had to leave the next week for the Michigan harvest.

"Right," she said not sure whether to be sad or thrilled. "Okay, this is Tuesday. We pick through Saturday, you rest on Sunday, we have the picnic on

Sunday night. You rest Monday, leave Tuesday. Sound okay?''

"Kate, you're too tired for a picnic this year."

"I'll have it catered. Sunday evening, Hector. No argument." She grinned. "It's been a good year."

He smiled. "For us, too," he said, and went to tell the other workers.

She wondered where she would ever find the energy to throw a picnic. But it was a tradition, and she wasn't about to cancel it. When she went to give Jay the schedule, he was working on the harvester belts.

"You mean on Sunday we actually get to sit down?" He wiped his sweating face with his bandanna. "I'll try to get everything picked while we have shed help."

She knew he was exhausted, but there was something else, something she couldn't put her finger on. He seemed as withdrawn as he was in those first days. "Are you okay?" she ventured.

"Yeah, I'm fine. Why?"

"You look…I don't know." The shadowy smile he gave her bothered her even more.

"It's nothing. Should I take it as a good sign that you're worried about me?"

She reached out a tentative hand to touch his face, and even though her body was running on automatic pilot, she felt a charge run down her arm. "Yeah, you should. We made it, Jay. Sunday…" She let her voice trail off, waiting for some sign from him.

"Yeah," he said tiredly, and went back to work.

Kate returned to the field with the gnawing feeling that something was terribly wrong, but with too little energy to do anything about it.

Sunday dawned hot and bright. Kate made a face at the clock, knowing she didn't have to get up. She was still tired, but it was a different kind of tired, what she called "after it's over" tired. She and Leonard had taken the last load of fresh berries to Tulsa the night before. She hadn't wanted to go, hadn't wanted him to go, but he was determined to take one load out. She'd gone with him to make sure he didn't unload the truck or do anything he shouldn't. When they got back at midnight, the shed was clean and most of the equipment was packed up for next year.

Now all she had to do today was get a picnic ready for sixty or seventy people. She usually barbecued chicken, but it had been a good year, so she'd made arrangements with a local barbecue place. All she had to do was organize things. Jay had bought a keg of beer, the women would fix tons of tortillas—the kind she could never get enough of—and she would fix some fruit. The thought of even that much work made her want to roll over and go back to sleep.

When she finally wandered down the stairs at about nine, her mother was in the kitchen peeling carrots. Snit sat beside her, snagging an occasional peeling and flinging it to the floor. "Mom, what are you doing?"

"Just adding a little color—and nutrition—to the party. Maria's making salsa. And I got the ingredients for the candy. Which you need to get busy on."

Kate groaned. Blueberry candy was a tradition for the kids. "At least the catering truck will arrive at the appointed time and disgorge a ton of delicious food without us having to turn a hand." She grabbed a carrot stick to munch. "Dad still asleep?"

Sarah nodded. "He had a wonderful time last night."

"I know. I let him drive all the way over. Said I was too tired." Sarah set cereal and juice in front of her. "So have you two decided what you're going to do? I assume Florida is out."

"You assume right. But Leonard's come through the harvest just fine, what with everyone watching out for him. We may buy that place up the road."

"That would be great, Mom. But you know you can stay here."

"You have your own life. Besides," she said, pointing a carrot at Snit, "I'll not share a kitchen with the empress here."

Her mother probably assumed that Jay would be moving in. The thought warmed her all over. "Mom, do you think Jay could ever be happy so far from Luke?"

Sarah looked at her daughter for a long moment. "I think it'd be tough, but yes, I think it could be done. Are you still worried?"

Kate played with her cereal. "Not for me. I'm worried for him. Getting pulled in too many directions."

"Well, you'll just have to work it out together. That's how these things are done."

"But what if Luther doesn't get well enough to—"

Sarah clamped a hand on her daughter's mouth. "And what if the sky falls, Chicken Little? Lord, you're worse than your father."

Several hours later, tables and chairs were set up under the sycamore trees near the lake. The little kids and teenagers were swimming and splashing. The men were relaxing, drinking beer and talking about the Michigan crop. The women gossiped and laughed and set food on the tables.

Kate made a dozen trips back to the house for things she'd forgotten. Each time she returned, she scanned the lake for Luke, the clusters of men for Jay, but neither were in sight. When the barbecue arrived, she finally asked if anyone had seen them.

One of the women looked up from the food table. "He and the boy left last night while we were cleaning the shed."

Jimmy Sanchez handed her a piece of paper. "I found this on his trailer."

She looked at the note through a blur of tears. "Family emergency. Call you tomorrow. Jay."

"He tried to find you," Rose said. "We told him you went to Tulsa. He said he couldn't wait. He looked crazy. *Muy loco*."

"Probably his dad," Kate said, but Luther was almost fully recovered from his stroke. Had he had a relapse? Had something happened with Luke? Kate shrugged and set a smile on her face.

Somehow she got through the rest of the afternoon, through the blur of goodbyes, hugs and promises for next year, but above it all, the sky *was* falling. What could be so important that he couldn't wait? So important he couldn't take time to explain in his note. Or had he just taken the easy way out? But she couldn't believe that. When she spoke to her mother, Sarah hugged her and told her to quit worrying.

"It's probably poor Luther. Strokes tend to visit a body more than once, honey."

Kate blinked back tears. A stroke meant . . . Luther wouldn't be coming. It meant no more ties to Arkansas. Now, the only question was whether Jay would ask her to come to California.

What if it isn't a stroke? a voice nagged. "If it isn't," she murmured, "then it's me." She tried to push aside the awful realization that on a hot sunny day in July the man she loved had just up and left.

CHAPTER TWELVE

THE NEXT DAY came and went, and the only phone calls were from people wanting blueberries. "We don't know what the situation is," her mother said. "Luther's condition could be critical."

"Yeah. But I can't believe I screwed up so royally. I had to put everything off till after harvest. I had to make sure everything was perfect."

"Honey, you're making a mountain out of a molehill. Jay wouldn't have left like that if he didn't have a good reason."

"Yeah, like being worn out from wasting his time on a twit like me."

"He'll call."

Gladys phoned every day to find out if they'd heard anything. "I can't imagine what could have happened," she said. "It must be grave, indeed. Now, when did you have in mind to get married, dear? I need plenty of notice."

"Gladys!" Kate railed.

"Nonsense. You may think he's abandoned us, but I've never lost a man once he's eaten my gravy."

"Probably looking for an airplane for us while he's out there," her father mused.

"Probably couldn't stand all this clean air," George grumped.

She knew they were all trying to make her feel better, but it wasn't working.

She hung around the house for the next three days, ostensibly resting, but jumping every time the phone rang. On the fourth day, she let the machine take all calls and went to the field to do some summer pruning, and to think and to get away from Gladys and her mom's cheerleading efforts.

Kate looked up at the bright summer sky and mopped her face with a bandanna. So many changes in one week. Jay and Luke were off heaven knew where. Her mother and father had decided to buy the little place down the road and were busy planning the remodeling. The farm was quiet again except for the sound of mowing and the hiss of irrigation lines feeding their lifesaving liquid to the plants. The plants didn't really need pruning, but it was hard, mind-numbing work that would leave her exhausted at night. Too exhausted to think of the seven days that had passed with no word from Jay. Too exhausted to condemn herself for letting him go without telling him she loved him.

Even after a day's work in the heat, sleep was fleeting in the long hours before dawn. She replayed the summer again and again, changing the scenes so the end came out right and happy.

The farm lay dull and burnished from the summer heat as it had lain each and every year after harvest. As if a man named Jay had never come and gone, except in her heart—which would never be the same.

Her mother kept saying he'd be back, although Kate thought she heard less conviction in those words with each passing day. Gladys was ranting and raving and threatening to go after him. Kate had believed he would be back at first. But as the days crept by, she had to assume that he had tired of waiting for some word from her, that he had finally understood he couldn't leave his son in California in the fall, couldn't drag his sick father out to the rigors of a farm operation. That he had discovered after the grueling harvest that blueberries were not what he wanted to do with the rest of his life. That... She had come up with a million explanations for why he had gone, and none of them ended with his coming back—or with her going out there.

Just like Toby. She tried to push that gut-wrenching thought aside, but it hovered like a dark cloud. Two differences. Toby hadn't made it through harvest, but he'd called. Jay had made it through harvest with flying colors, then...

She'd even dialed Beth's number, convinced that something had happened to Luther, but the answering machine told her nothing. So she tended her farm and the big farm, and waited, expecting a For Sale sign to go up any day.

GEORGE SHOULDERED his loppers. "Too damn hot out here, missy. I'm goin' home."

"It is a tad warm today, isn't it?"

"Warm, my foot. July and August in Arkansas is a test of how a man's gonna fare in hell. You best get to the house, too, missy."

"I will in a little while." A faint drone sounded from the direction of the river, and Kate looked up to see a small plane buzz over the treetops, then glide in a lazy circle over the farm.

George shaded his eyes. "What's that fool think he's doin'?"

"Probably the sheriff's plane looking for marijuana plants."

"Well, he oughtta know better than to look here."

"It's that time of year. They always check the river."

The plane flew low, wagged its wings three times and made a beeline for town. George ambled toward the house and Kate bent to her pruning.

An hour later she decided the heat was too much even for her. She was on her way to the house when she saw the man standing at the end of the row watching her. She stopped and pulled down the brim of her hat another notch to shade her eyes. He was tall and broad-shouldered. An unruly shock of black hair ruffled in the hot wind. She thought for a moment it was Jay, but... Heat rippled and his image wavered, lost in the tears that filled her eyes and heart. She shook her head, unsure of what she was seeing.

But when she looked up again, he was still there, and now he was walking toward her. She blinked, but he kept coming.

She threw down the loppers and broke into a run. And when he gathered her in his arms, she knew he was real.

"I thought you were a mirage!" she gasped.

"I thought you were going to turn and walk the other way," he murmured, smothering her with kisses.

She leaned into him, savoring his scent, his strength. "I thought you were gone for good because I was so stupid. Why didn't you call?"

Jay held her at arm's length, frowning. "What are you talking about?"

"I thought you'd just up and left because you got tired of waiting. I thought..."

He tipped her hat back. "How could you ever think I'd do something like that, Kate?"

Looking at him, she couldn't imagine. "I don't know, I just did. Dammit, why didn't you call?"

Jay nodded toward the end of the field. Kate saw an older man wave. "Is that . . . ?"

"It is. Luther Thomas in the flesh. I've been chasing him all over the western half of the country."

"Chasing?"

"Come on. It's too hot out here to talk." He took her hand and led her out of the field. "When you and Leonard drove to Tulsa last week, I got a frantic call from Beth. She'd been telling me for several days that Dad was up to something, but she didn't know what. That's why I was so distracted that last week."

"You could have told me."

He kissed her hand. "You were about ready to drop. You didn't need that. Anyway, it seems that Dad was determined to make at least the tail end of the harvest. He hijacked Beth's car and took off. We had no idea what route he'd taken, but we banked on it being the same one he'd taken before. I was ready to call out the National Guard when I finally caught up with him in Colorado. I ditched the cars and rented a plane to get us back."

Kate clapped a hand over her mouth. "That sounds like something Daddy would do."

"I worry about those two together. There's no telling what they'll get into, left unsupervised."

Suddenly Kate noticed the older man standing some distance away. "Luther," she called. "You're a little late, but we can probably find *something* for you to pick."

"Wasn't my idea," he called back, and walked toward them. He looked exactly the way he had the year before except for a slight limp in his left leg. He hugged Kate. "By the time I stole Beth's car, it was too late to get here."

"I can't believe you did that," Kate said. "Where's Luke?"

Luther smiled. "Asleep in the car. He's had the time of his life this week. Thought he was in the middle of a cops-and-robbers TV show."

Jay cuffed his father gently on the shoulder. "I'm glad somebody had fun. Next time I'll leave you for the coyotes. Now go find Leonard and Sarah so I can talk to my woman."

Luther winked and slowly walked out of the field. Jay led Kate to the shade of the oak tree near the stand. He made her sit down and knelt in front of her.

"I kept meaning to call, but I was frantic. I was sure he was in a ditch somewhere in the middle of nowhere. And I had Luke and..." He searched her eyes. "Oh, Kate, it never occurred to me that you would think I wasn't coming back."

"I wouldn't have blamed you." She touched her fingers to his lips. "I was afraid you'd gotten tired of waiting for me to tell you how much I love you."

"Katherine Ann Harmon, do you know how long I've waited to hear that?" He leaned forward and kissed her. "I'd already made up my mind to marry you whether you wanted to or not."

"Good grief, you sound like Barry."

"I had it all planned out. If I moved here and you had to look at me every day, eventually I'd wear you down. You'd have to forgive me sooner or later."

She touched his cheek. "There was never anything to forgive. Except my pride."

"So we're okay, farmer lady?"

"We're okay," she vowed, and sealed it with a kiss.

He stood and pulled her to her feet. "The first order of business is to go hog-tie our fathers before they take off for parts unknown. Probably in a stolen airplane."

She reached up for another kiss. "We made it through the season, Jay."

"That we did. And I heard from a very reliable source that Jennifer is keeping company with a jet-setter in Monaco."

"You think there's a chance..."

He crossed his fingers and held them high. "Just maybe. But if it doesn't, Luke loves planes. Now are you going to tell Gladys or am I?"

"Oh, Lord, she'll buy up all the food in this county and we'll have to eat it."

"We'll buy lots of freezers." He kissed her again, his lips lingering on hers. "You know, I think I got the first order of business all wrong...."

As he pulled her back down to the warm grass, she heard something she'd never heard before—an owl calling in broad daylight. And then she heard his mate answer.

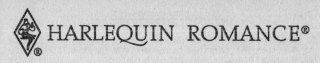

HARLEQUIN ROMANCE®

Coming Next Month

#3327 ITALIAN INVADER Jessica Steele
Working for Max Zappelli has become more and more confusing for
Elyn Talbot. Her family believes he's responsible for the collapse of their
company, she believes he's an incorrigible womanizer, and he believes she's
a thief. And to complicate things further, Elyn is falling in love with the
irresistible Max.

#3328 THE DINOSAUR LADY Anne Marie Duquette
Jason Reilly *loves* dinosaurs. And he's crazy about Denver's Dinosaur Lady—
paleontologist and TV host Noel Forrest. He's actually got a fossil—he's *sure*
it's a dinosaur bone—to show Noel. He found it on Matt Caldwell's ranch,
where he's been going for recreational therapy ever since the accident that
left him crippled. Jason no longer has a family of his own, and he thinks Matt
and Noel would be the *perfect* parents for him. Now, if only he could get them
together....
This is our fourth Kids & Kisses title. Next month, watch for *Sullivan's Law*
by Amanda Clark.

#3329 THE CONFIRMED BACHELOR Ellen James
Rebecca Danley's a die-hard romantic. The way she figures it, you meet a
wonderful man, fall in love with him and want to have his kids…in that order.
Unfortunately, she's gotten things all turned around. She's become obsessed
with the idea of having children. Even worse, the only man in her life is a
confirmed bachelor!

#3330 AN IMPOSSIBLE KIND OF MAN Kay Gregory
Slade *was* impossible. Impossible to ignore! Especially now that Bronwen's
forced to share his apartment. But Bronwen still thinks she can ignore the
attraction she feels for him. And if the inevitable happens, she can always
count on Slade to do the honorable thing. *Can't she?*

AVAILABLE THIS MONTH:

#3323 AT ODDS WITH LOVE
Betty Neels

#3325 BRIDE OF MY HEART
Rebecca Winters

#3324 FAMILY SECRETS
Leigh Michaels

#3326 ON BLUEBERRY HILL
Marcella Thompson

MILLION DOLLAR SWEEPSTAKES (III)

No purchase necessary. To enter, follow the directions published. Method of entry may vary. For eligibility, entries must be received no later than March 31, 1996. No liability is assumed for printing errors, lost, late or misdirected entries. Odds of winning are determined by the number of eligible entries distributed and received. Prizewinners will be determined no later than June 30, 1996.

Sweepstakes open to residents of the U.S. (except Puerto Rico), Canada, Europe and Taiwan who are 18 years of age or older. All applicable laws and regulations apply. Sweepstakes offer void wherever prohibited by law. Values of all prizes are in U.S. currency. This sweepstakes is presented by Torstar Corp., its subsidiaries and affiliates, in conjunction with book, merchandise and/or product offerings. For a copy of the Official Rules send a self-addressed, stamped envelope (WA residents need not affix return postage) to: MILLION DOLLAR SWEEPSTAKES (III) Rules, P.O. Box 4573, Blair, NE 68009, USA.

EXTRA BONUS PRIZE DRAWING

No purchase necessary. The Extra Bonus Prize will be awarded in a random drawing to be conducted no later than 5/30/96 from among all entries received. To qualify, entries must be received by 3/31/96 and comply with published directions. Drawing open to residents of the U.S. (except Puerto Rico), Canada, Europe and Taiwan who are 18 years of age or older. All applicable laws and regulations apply; offer void wherever prohibited by law. Odds of winning are dependent upon number of eligible entries received. Prize is valued in U.S. currency. The offer is presented by Torstar Corp., its subsidiaries and affiliates in conjunction with book, merchandise and/or product offering. For a copy of the Official Rules governing this sweepstakes, send a self-addressed, stamped envelope (WA residents need not affix return postage) to: Extra Bonus Prize Drawing Rules, P.O. Box 4590, Blair, NE 68009, USA.

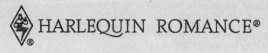

HARLEQUIN ROMANCE®

brings you

Stories that celebrate love, families and children!

Watch for our next Kids & Kisses title in September.

The Dinosaur Lady
by Anne Marie Duquette
Harlequin Romance #3328

A Romance that will move you and thrill you! By the author of **Rescued by Love, On the Line** *and* **Neptune's Bride.**

Noelle Forrest is "the Dinosaur Lady." Jason Reilly is the eleven-year-old boy who brings her a dinosaur fossil that may be her biggest career break ever—a fossil he found on Matt Caldwell's ranch.

Noelle discovers that there's room in her life and heart for more than just her career. There's room for Jason, who hasn't got a real family of his own—and for Matt, a strong compassionate man who thinks children are more important than dinosaurs....

Available wherever Harlequin books are sold.

HARLEQUIN®

Weddings, Inc.

THE WEDDING GAMBLE
Muriel Jensen

Eternity, Massachusetts, was America's wedding town. Paul Bertrand knew this better than anyone—he never should have gotten soused at his friend's rowdy bachelor party. Next morning when he woke up, he found he'd somehow managed to say "I do"—to the woman he'd once jilted! And Christina Bowman had helped launch so many honeymoons, she knew just what to do on theirs!

THE WEDDING GAMBLE, available in September from American Romance, is the fourth book in Harlequin's new cross-line series, **WEDDINGS, INC.**

Be sure to look for the fifth book, **THE VENGEFUL GROOM,** by Sara Wood (Harlequin Presents #1692), coming in October.

WED4

HARLEQUIN®

Don't miss these Harlequin favorites by some of our most distinguished authors!
And now you can receive a discount by ordering two or more titles!

HT #25525	THE PERFECT HUSBAND by Kristine Rolofson	$2.99	☐
HT #25554	LOVERS' SECRETS by Glenda Sanders	$2.99	– ☐
HP #11577	THE STONE PRINCESS by Robyn Donald	$2.99	☐
HP #11554	SECRET ADMIRER by Susan Napier	$2.99	☐
HR #03277	THE LADY AND THE TOMCAT by Bethany Campbell	$2.99	☐
HR #03283	FOREIGN AFFAIR by Eva Rutland	$2.99	☐
HS #70529	KEEPING CHRISTMAS by Marisa Carroll	$3.39	☐
HS #70578	THE LAST BUCCANEER by Lynn Erickson	$3.50	☐
HI #22256	THRICE FAMILIAR by Caroline Burnes	$2.99	☐
HI #22238	PRESUMED GUILTY by Tess Gerritsen	$2.99	☐
HAR #16496	OH, YOU BEAUTIFUL DOLL by Judith Arnold	$3.50	☐
HAR #16510	WED AGAIN by Elda Minger	$3.50	☐
HH #28719	RACHEL by Lynda Trent	$3.99	☐
HH #28795	PIECES OF SKY by Marianne Willman	$3.99	☐

Harlequin Promotional Titles

#97122	LINGERING SHADOWS by Penny Jordan	$5.99	☐
	(limited quantities available on certain titles)		

	AMOUNT	$
DEDUCT:	10% DISCOUNT FOR 2+ BOOKS	$
	POSTAGE & HANDLING	$
	($1.00 for one book, 50¢ for each additional)	
	APPLICABLE TAXES*	$_____
	TOTAL PAYABLE	$_____
	(check or money order—please do not send cash)	

To order, complete this form and send it, along with a check or money order for the total above, payable to Harlequin Books, to: **In the U.S.:** 3010 Walden Avenue, P.O. Box 9047, Buffalo, NY 14269-9047; **In Canada:** P.O. Box 613, Fort Erie, Ontario, L2A 5X3.

Name: _____

Address:_____City: _____

State/Prov.: _____ Zip/Postal Code: _____

*New York residents remit applicable sales taxes.
 Canadian residents remit applicable GST and provincial taxes..

HBACK-JS